Show Pony

Show Pony

Chris Craig

Copyright © 2011, 2012 by Christopher R. Craig

All rights reserved. Printed in the United States of America. No part of this book may be used or reproduced in any manner whatsoever without written permission from the author and publisher, except in the case of a reviewer who may quote brief passages in a review. For information write:

OR Louie Press
2554 W. Logan Blvd. Suite 202
Chicago, IL 60647

The characters and events in this book are fictitious. Any similarity to real persons, living or dead, is purely coincidental and not intended by the author.

ISBN 978-0-557-83311-5

for Phoebe, for everything

1

The Hawaiian Breeze Motor Lodge was on Highway 41 just outside Evansville, Indiana. The place had about as much to do with Hawaii as Indiana did with pineapples and hula girls. The child size coffee maker on the bathroom counter coughed and sputtered the last drop of my breakfast into the tiny pot. I played with the steam on the mirror and waited for the rusty water running from the busted shower head to clear. There was a knock on the door.

"You want room service?"

"No thanks."

"Clean towels?"

I walked over and opened the door. It was Wanda, the maid. She stood there smoking her cigarette as though she had some kind of higher purpose. Repeated cheap dye jobs had dried out her hair and the tattoos on her hands looked as though they were of the county lockup variety. She could have been an NFL linebacker had it not been for the enormous breasts that hung beneath her Destin, Florida t-shirt.

"Bet you at least could use some clean sheets." She gave me a wink and nod. Two silver caps outshone the rest of her beige teeth.

"Nobody's been in here but me, Wanda."

"We can change that honey," she said, her heavy smoker laugh made her cough.

"I'm flattered, really," I said, "but it wouldn't be fair to your hardworking man at home."

"Shit, that loser?" Wanda looked at me for a second longer inhaling her smoke. "Take some toilet paper leastways." She tossed me a roll.

"Thanks. I'll use it to sand down the furniture." Wanda exhaled a plume of blue smoke and nodded knowingly then rolled her cart away.

The paper cups the motel supplied were so cheap they could barely hold warm water. The coffee pot was no larger than a mug. I dumped some artificial sweetener into it and took a sip. It was lousy as expected. I decided to smoke one of Wanda's cigarettes.

I had been staying at the Hawaiian for the past few days. She had left them in my room the first day she cleaned it. We talked for a while, mostly small talk. She said people didn't stay in dives like the Hawaiian for long, mostly tired truckers or lonely businessmen with hookers. She was fishing, waiting for my story, wanted to know what my plan was. Truth was I didn't have a plan, not one I had told anyone anyway. I sat on the bed and enjoyed my weak coffee.

The TV got two channels. One was a network affiliate broadcasting the local news and the other featured a war movie with a young Ernest Borgnine. I shut it off. I looked at my phone, my silent friend, and waited for something to happen. After thirty-two years of being stuck in the same place, I found myself somewhere else, thinking not only of how I got there, but wondering where I would go.

You can only run so far in the same pair of shoes, tell the same joke so many times, sing the same song to the same girl for so many years before your shit runs thin. My shoes needed new soles. I wasn't funny anymore and the song I chose was never really that good to begin with. I opened the drawer to the nightstand and looked in at the Holy Bible left by the Gideons. The black cover was pristine, its red edged pages untouched. I didn't need to read it. It was just a comfort knowing it was there.

2

A few weeks earlier I was in the Briarfield Elks Club sipping a cold beer and playing Golden Tee. I stood in front of the machine not knowing what to feel worse about, that I was screwing one of my students or the fact that I didn't care. On top of that I was most likely going to lose my job and close the final chapter on a failed marriage.

We have visions in our heads when we are younger of who we think we will become, what we will look like, where we will live. I was right where I thought I would be, nowhere, in Briarfield, Illinois.

The pixelated numbers flashed the countdown on the screen. I fumbled in my pocket for two quarters, shoved them into the game and resumed my round. I had never played a real game of golf before, but that day I was shooting a course record fifteen under par at Augusta and the crowd was going wild. I wondered what it would be like to be a golf pro, traveling to the most beautiful locales in the world, playing golf in all that sunny weather, signing autographs, cashing endorsement checks, waving to the fans. My concentration waned on my third shot on 18. The ball plunked into the front of the sand trap.

"Shit!" I smacked the machine.

"Just a game, Davenport," Wes, the bartender said. He wiped his forehead with the bar towel that hung over his shoulder and chewed on a red cocktail straw.

"All I needed was a birdie on the last hole for the course record."

"And then what? You type your initials next to your score? Big deal."

You needed to carry an umbrella when you talked to Wes. He loved pissing on people's parades.

"I forgot that you suck at this game," I said.

"Yep. You wanna another beer?"

"No. I got some work to do."

Wes walked out from the back of the bar over to the video poker game. "How'd you do on this?" Wes looked at the screen then wrote down the number of credits on a clipboard that was tied to the back of the machine. "Ah, the sweet kiss of Lady Luck." He walked back behind the bar, hit the cash register and handed me a twenty. "Don't blow it all in one place."

I took the bill. "I'll be handing it back to you in a few hours." Neither of us laughed. We both knew I wasn't kidding.

3

I walked down the lonesome aisles of storage units like a prison guard after lights out. The blacktop undulated in places. Puddles from the afternoon rain rested in the shallow pockets left by the uneven indentations. I had seen flatter lines on the tops of hand pressed rice krispie treats, but that is what you get when you decide to save a few bucks and do things yourself.

I had forty sheds on the property surrounded by razor wire, guarded with an electric gate and an access code system. The sheds ranged from thirty-five to fifty dollars a month in rent depending on the square footage. Provided the lot was rented out I made a tidy fifteen hundred and fifty dollars a month. That netted a nice annual sum of eighteen thousand and six hundred dollars. Add in the seven grand I made teaching art at Pioneer Community College and I was doing okay considering where I lived.

Briarfield was a small town of five thousand people. Most of the tenants I rented to were older and stored anything from old magazines and antiques to appliances and seasonal clothing. I made sure all the sheds were locked. If I noticed a latch was rusted or needed replacing I jotted down the unit number in my notebook.

I did all of the bookkeeping in a small office I kept up front by the gate. It was simple accounting really. I had a list of names down one side of the ledger and the different months across the top. Once a person mailed in their check for the month I put an x by their name. I had a two week grace period, then a twenty dollar late fee. If they were two months late I made a phone call, after that I charged the amount to their credit card. I was my own boss, owned the business and insurance covered the rest. Other than teaching, it was a perfect job for a painter. I had plenty of time to mess with the canvas and there was virtually no overhead.

You could tell a lot about a person by looking in their closet. Sheds were different. You couldn't really tell much by looking in a shed. Maybe pull out a hobby or two, but for the most part people stored things in sheds that they didn't want or couldn't fit in their homes. Provided it wasn't illegal, it wasn't any of my business what people stored at my place. Unless I was on site while people were loading or unloading their things, I rarely ever knew what kind of shit they kept.

I walked on through the ghost town of sheds. It wasn't until I got to the end of the row that I heard the generator. I took a deep breath through my nose for meth fumes, nothing. I looked around then saw the padlock on number thirty had been removed. I banged on the retractable metal door.

"It's open."

I pulled the door up and shook my head. Jasper Sullivan, eighty-two, was sitting in a bean bag chair eating corn chips and watching the St. Louis Cardinals play the Cubs.

"Jas, we talked about this bullshit. What gives?"

"Huh?" He pointed at the loud generator.

"What are you doing in here?" I yelled.

"Opening day. Myron wanted to watch some dumbass game show."

Myron was Jasper's roommate at the assisted living facility a mile down the road. Jasper was a retired soybean farmer. His wife and kids still lived in town. He was in the early stages of Alzheimer's.

"You know if you got struck by lightning out here I could lose the whole business. My insurance coverage is for inanimate objects only, not Cardinal fans."

"It's enough I got to sleep in a place that smells like piss, surrounded by rude nurses, now you're kicking me out of my own shed?"

"I'm worried about your safety."

"Your granddad would box your ears if he knew you were hasslin' me on opening day."

Jasper and my deceased grandfather, Walter, were old fishing buddies, lifetime Cardinals fans and WWII vets.

"So how are you getting home?"

"Cab after the game."

"Alright then, be careful. I don't feel too good about this."

"Live on the edge a little, Roarke. It's good for ya."

I looked at Jasper and walked on. A few moments later I turned around and walked back to the shed. "We don't have any cabs in Briarfield."

"This game is over in just a few more innings."

I reached over to turn off the generator when Jasper's crotchety expression melted into that of a child. His jacket was open and his shirt was unbuttoned in random areas. The yellowed t-shirt beneath it was as thin as gauze. White strands of long wispy hair were plastered across his head and his boots had mud on them.

"Did you walk here?"

"I keep the code scratched inside my belt." He smiled like a proud kid in an old man's tired body. It was bullshit how his family had deserted him. Whatever had occurred in his family's past his wife had completely washed her hands of.

"Does anybody know you're here?"

"Myron does, but he zips it pretty good when I give him my meds." Jasper crunched on a few more corn chips. A Cub rounded the bases following his solo shot onto Waveland. "Sonofabitch!"

"I'll be right back." I went to my car and opened the cooler I kept in the back. Two dented sixteen-ounce tall boys rested on their sides from an excursion two days prior. The ice in the cooler had melted, but the water that surrounded the cans was still cold. I grabbed the cans and walked back to Jasper's shed.

"You want a beer to go with your chips?"

"Can't. Claire says beer makes me an asshole." Claire was Jasper's wife.

"You don't live with Claire anymore. You live with Myron Apples in an old folks home." Jasper stared at me blankly. "You've been living there for a few years now."

"I think I hate it there don't I?"

"You do."

"Why am I stuck there again?"

"Your wife put you there."

"But she's coming back to get me right?"

"I don't know, buddy."

I opened one of the cans and handed it to Jasper. Then I opened mine and took a healthy swig. Not bad. I grabbed a handful of the old man's corn chips.

"Who's winning?" I said.

"Who cares?"

I sat down on the concrete floor next to Jasper in his bean bag chair. We watched the images flicker on the television screen while the generator ran like a locomotive chasing the afternoon sun.

4

I returned home to the small farmhouse I rented. I had been living there for a year and a half since the split with my wife, Denise. It had two rooms and a kitchen. I slept in one room and used the other as a studio for my painting. A dim lamp in the corner revealed various silhouettes of numerous canvases in different stages of completion. In front of the easels and canvases were various tubes of paint, oily rags and thinner. An upside down metal trash can lid nailed to a lazy susan served as my palette.

I walked into the kitchen and got a glass of water then walked back out and had a seat on my sunken sofa. I looked at the portrait I was doing of my grandfather then the one I was working on of my mom. The similarities in their features were undeniable, but the technique I used in painting each of them was totally different. Slow, steady, and deliberate strokes created Walter's face, while erratic and untamed squiggles and flurries of color made up the face of my mom. Their eyes looked out in the same way, the same stubborn gaze. Of the same blood, their lives couldn't have been more different. I wondered if they could see the same things now, perhaps in the same way.

Amanda Renae Davenport was sixteen years old when she gave birth to me. "Wilder than a horse and prettier than a flower," was how my grandmother, Gladys, described her in her high school days.

"Crazier than hell and dumb enough not to care," was what Walter said.

Walter sold insurance, or as he put it, "peace of mind." His favorite animal was the squirrel because of its preparedness. "Nuts for the winter," he'd always say when he was heading to the bank. Walter worked so hard on helping other people guard against catastrophe and prepare for disaster that he never had time to really focus on his own family.

One morning, while my mom waited for her boyfriend to pick her up for high school, she informed Walter and Gladys that she wanted to change her name to Dandelion.

"Holy shit! Our only child is a grass-smoking hippie."

"Walter!" Gladys said.

"Oregano my ass." Walter took a sip of coffee.

Mom ran out the door without hearing any of it. A few months later she announced she was pregnant.

Dandelion took off when I was five months old. She left a note on the kitchen table saying she still had a lot of living to do before she felt she could raise a kid. She was leaving Briarfield to "discover herself and realize her dreams." She was hitchhiking to California and was going to become a model. Gladys told me that as soon as Walter had read the note he handed me over to her and went and put on a cowboy hat and a jacket.

"Where are you going?" Gladys asked.

"Well hell, if it's dream time, I'm off to Montana to be a cowboy." After that Gladys said Walter didn't talk for a week.

5

I went to a lot of church socials and Rotary functions with Walter and Gladys. I attended more than my fair share of funerals and volunteered down at the VFW with them. By the time I was seven I had become quite the bridge player and had my own variations on how to make a green bean casserole. Walter and I never won any three-legged races at the Father/Son picnic for Scouts, nor did Gladys bake the best chocolate chip cookies, but I knew in their hearts they were trying their best to give me a normal childhood.

They didn't tell me everything when I was a kid. They didn't have to. I had a pretty good idea of what was going on. Like most kids, I could sense things, feel out situations; understand the score without having to watch the entire game.

Every few months Dandelion would pass through town and visit me. After she and Walter went a few rounds, she'd take me to the Dairy Queen for our traditional snack of french fries and a Coke. She was so thin, but we always shared food because she was constantly "running low on bread." I walked over to the playground in the front of the restaurant.

"So how are ole Walt and Glad?" Dandelion asked, eating the fries as though she were being timed in a competition.

"Pretty good," I said, swinging upside down from the monkey bars by one leg, hoping to impress her. "He's teaching me to mow the lawn and paint the garage."

"Jesus, you're his grandson not his slave."

"I like learning stuff from him."

"Seems wrong to me. Ordering you around, taking advantage of you." I walked up and over the steel jungle gym without using my hands. A small smattering of applause broke out as other concerned parents yelled at a clueless Dandelion. "Say, do you still have that two-dollar bill I gave you last time I visited?" I dropped down to the ground and dug around in my Velcro wallet.

"Yeah. Why?"

"Let's get some cheeseburgers."

"But those are my nuts for the winter."

Dandelion rolled her eyes. "Just cause you live there doesn't mean you have to talk like him too."

We sat in a booth while Dandelion ate the cheeseburgers. She told me how terrible Walter and Gladys were to her growing up. How she wanted to be a model, but they weren't supportive.

"If they are so bad why'd you leave me with them?" I asked.

Dandelion looked at me. "I got a crazy schedule, kiddo. No room for a kid on the road. Unfortunately, it's the price we gotta pay for me to make it."

That night Dandelion brought me home late. Walter was waiting in his pajamas.

"Where in the hell have you been?"

Gladys studied Dandelion. "She's not drunk, dear."

"Of course I'm not. Don't scold me in front of Roarke."

"Take it easy, Amanda, have a seat and let's talk," Gladys said.

"My name is Dandelion."

"Oh sweet Mary, here we go with the Dandelion shit," Walter said.

"Don't swear or talk to me like that in front of my kid."

"Your kid? When is the last time you bought him any clothes or helped him with his homework?"

"How dare you lecture me about being a parent when you never listened to a word I said when I was growing up."

"Growing up? When did you do that? Hell, you were a stupid kid when you left."

"Honestly, Walter, please," Gladys said.

"Quiet mom," Dandelion said, "and for the last time my name is Dandelion."

"What's wrong with Amanda?" Gladys asked.

"Dandelion symbolizes growth and beauty anywhere."

"You really ought to get off the dope," Walter said.

"A dandelion is a weed, a nuisance." Gladys began to cry.

Dandelion stood still for a moment and looked at Walter. "You said it." She walked over and kissed me on top of my head, then walked out the door.

6

Weeks went by since Dandelion had bolted and still no word from her. The whole thing made Walter nervous, but he didn't talk about it with me, didn't say a single word. Occasionally I would notice tears in Gladys' eyes, but she would turn as soon as she saw me. When she would talk to me it was only surface conversation like "supper is ready" or "time for bed." Silence is a powerful thing. It can be used as a weapon or a defense, and with Walter I never knew how he intended it. Gladys told me one day that she was sorry she had been so quiet, that she was depressed.

"Depressed?"

"Being deeply blue about the state of things," she said.

"So like my clothes then?" I looked down at the yellow and brown patterned shirt with fake pearl buttons and uneven sleeves. My corduroy pants had a denim patch over one knee.

"Not really," Gladys chuckled, "Those are pretty sad though."

"Dandelion made them for me."

Gladys sobbed, "I taught her to sew better than that."

"Is Walter depressed?"

"Yes," she said. "He's sad and very angry."

Walter put all of his worry and nervous energy into busy work and chores around the house. Refilling the birdfeeder meant taking the whole thing apart, sanding and repainting it. He planted an herb garden, reorganized the garage and built a deck on the back of the house.

A few more weeks passed and we started receiving postcards from Los Angeles and San Francisco from Dandelion. She told me how great her life was and how much fun she was having booking modeling jobs. She never mentioned the magazines she was in, but I always guessed that was because there wasn't room on the postcard. One day Walter pointed out to me that every postcard was postmarked from Edwardsville, Ill.

"What does that mean?" I said.

"It means your mother is a bad liar."

I felt bad for Dandelion and figured she must have not liked herself too much. Lying to me, hoping to make me proud? I didn't understand it. It seemed strange to me. Strange and nice at the same time and the thought of it made me sad and angry, like Walter.

7

Sometimes when I got lonely as a kid I would look at the other kids with their moms and dads, see them all playing and laughing and try to think what that would feel like. If I was at the pool I'd close my eyes and picture being thrown around in the pool by my dad, or if I was at the park I would imagine what it would be like playing Frisbee with Dandelion. Sometimes it actually worked and cheered me up. After awhile I just got used to having Walter and Gladys as my parents.

My dad took off before I was born. Never met him, but Walter did the best he could to explain the difficult and sensitive situation to me.

"He was a real shit heel, plain and simple, Roarke. Drove smash-up derby cars and loved pimento loaf."

"Was he funny?"

"Funny looking," Walter said. "He wore a dirty jean jacket and had huge bushy sideburns."

One day I watched an after school special about a man that didn't even know he had a son. Convinced that there had been a mistake in my situation, I rode my bike across town and out onto the interstate looking for my dad. I was in third grade. I thought he might see me pedaling in the hot sun, notice I looked just like him, then pull over and give me a ride. He'd say how sorry he was, and we'd laugh at how the whole crazy mix-up had occurred to begin with. By the third mile marker I didn't see a thing. I kept pedaling for as long as I could. I was sunburned and tired when a State Trooper picked me up.

"What ya doing out in this heat?" The Trooper asked, aiming an air-conditioned vent my way. It was my first time in a police cruiser. Normally, I would have been impressed by all the dials and gadgets, but I was spent.

"Looking for somebody," I said.

"Must be important, you riding your bike out on the highway."

"Yeah."

"What's his name? I'll put out an APB."

"What's an APB?"

"All points bulletin. It means for everyone to keep their eyes peeled."

I considered it for a moment. "Okay."

"Well, what's the name?" The Trooper asked.

"Of who?" I said.

"The name of the person you're looking for."

"I don't know his name. It's my dad."

The Trooper laughed. "How can you not know your own dad's name?" I felt the lump in my throat rise. "Where do you live buddy?"

When I got back to Walter and Gladys's house, Walter was out mowing the grass. He saw the patrol car, shut off the mower and slowly walked over. I looked at him, his hands had grease on them and his thinning hair was stuck to his sweaty forehead. He talked to the State Trooper for a bit, then unloaded my bike from the trunk of the cruiser. He shook the Trooper's hand and thanked him, then walked over to me.

"Long ride?"

"Yep."

"Where'd you go?"

"Highway." I said, my arms crossed.

"Highway? That's quite a ride for a little guy like you. You looking for something?"

"No." I felt tears well up in my eyes. I hated that he knew.

Walter squatted down next to me and looked me in the eye. "He's not worth finding, Roarke. He's not worth the sweat nor toil you put into that bike."

"Why'd he go?" I said sobbing.

"That's all some people know how to do." He mussed my hair and hugged me. It was the first time I could ever remember Walter doing that. "The way I see it you're lucky. Your great-grandfather, my dad, was a real asshole."

"Really?"

"Hell yeah," Walter said.

"Didn't he show up to your ball games?"

"Ball games? Those were for other people's kids. I stared at a horse's ass driving a plow all day long."

"Really?"

"Yeah."

"I bet he at least gave you birthday cards."

"Actually, back in those days people wished they hadn't been born. We were poor."

"Didn't you ever have a birthday cake?"

"My mother cooked a pan of cornbread for me one year and dad gave me a pocket knife."

"That's pretty neat."

"Nah, it wasn't sharp. Say, you want to have some fun?"

"Sure."

"Grab that rake and follow me around with the mower."

We worked on the lawn all afternoon, trimming, bagging, edging. It felt nice to have control over something. There was no mystery in lawn work. Just seeing what needed to be done and doing it. I remember dragging the metal teeth of the rake over the lawn and being grateful that the grass grew and that we needed to cut it. It felt nice to have a hand in something, to make a difference for the better no matter how small or short lived.

Some motorists drove by, honked their horns and waved to us while we worked. One after another they all sped on, different makes and models to different places.

8

The phone rang late one night. Walter answered it in his pajamas. It was either a wrong number or a crank call. I ran to the phone in the hallway. It was always fun to watch Walter give the person on the other end of the line one of his legendary dispatches. This time he just held the phone to his ear. "Amanda? Is that you?" Walter's pale hand gripped the receiver.

"Edwardsville?" Gladys asked.

"Springfield," Walter said. "Stay there and we will wire you the money," he said back into the phone. "Which Western Union?" He wrote down the info and hung up.

"Is she okay?" Gladys asked.

"Doped out of her mind," Walter said. He got dressed quickly and grabbed his keys.

"Be careful, dear."

"I'll be back." Walter stepped over and gave Gladys a kiss. He turned and looked at me. "Hold down the fort, Roarke," and with that he was gone. I remember feeling cool that he thought enough of me to ask me to hold down the fort. Gladys went over and grabbed her Bible.

"Come pray with me. Your mom is in a lot of trouble."

Walter returned with Dandelion the next day. Gladys and I both began sobbing as soon as we saw her. She was so skinny and pale and in such bad shape that we barely recognized her. She was weak. Her eyes had dark bags under them.

Walter carried Dandelion into my bedroom. I slept on the couch for the next few weeks. A doctor came to see her every few days. Gladys would make soup and let me take it to her. We'd try and help Dandelion eat it even though she didn't eat much. I'd read her sections of the newspaper and the funny pages and sometimes she smiled.

"Who was she with?" I asked Walter the next night. He was out in the garage stripping a rocking chair he had bought for Gladys at a yard sale. The man could not sit still. He always had to be working on something.

"A bad crew," Walter said. He worked on the chair as though it were his chosen profession. His right hand was cut up and swollen, but it didn't faze him. Walter turned and looked at me. His eyes looked as though he had been awake for days. He kept stripping the chair. I looked at his hands again. Pinkish-orange Merthiolate covered the cuts.

"What happened to your hands?"

"I had to swat a few pests."

"You got in a fight?"

"Look, your dear mother has flies stuck in her nose that cause her to be attracted to shit. We're going to clean her nose out and get her on the right track. You think you can help me do it?"

"Sure," I said. "Anything you need. Is she going to be okay?"

"Yeah," Walter said. "She's got a long way to go though." He kept working on the chair, peeling off layers and years of stain.

9

"This dress makes me look like such a square." Dandelion walked into the kitchen pulling on her sleeves.

"Well I think you look beautiful, honey," Gladys said.

"Your mother picked that out for you brand new, so you be nice." Gladys shot Walter a look.

I sat at the table eating my cold breakfast cereal. I wanted the sweetened kind with the colored marshmallows, but Walter said it would rot my teeth. Instead, I was eating a bowl of Walter's favorite, *Bran Blast*. "Slower to get to the bottom of that box, aren't you, fella?" He said, smiling over the corner of his paper.

"Yeah, there's no prize."

Walter furrowed his brow. "The prize is that you'll be more regular than a goose after a taco salad."

"Oh take it easy on him, Walt. He's only in third grade." Walter frowned and stared into the crease of his paper. "So what about you?" Dandelion asked looking at me. "How do I look?"

I looked at Dandelion and felt a tremendous swell of pride. She looked beautiful. She was no longer pale and thin with sunken eyes, but rather a healthy lady with a pretty dress on. She was wearing make-up and her hair was neatly styled and curled. I wanted to take a picture of her and keep it in my wallet.

"You look great!" I said.

Dandelion smiled. "This get-up doesn't make me look like a sell out to the man?"

No," I said laughing.

"Mary Mother, Amanda, you're going to have to lose the hippie-speak at the office. I'm running an insurance company, not a love in," Walter said.

More hard looks from Gladys.

"Take it easy, old timer," Dandelion said. She walked over to the coffee pot and poured herself a cup. "I'm stepping out for a cigarette. Ready when you are."

Gladys looked at Walter and closed her eyes in prayer. Dandelion blew me a kiss. "Do good at school and don't take any shit."

Walter's brow furrowed again. Dandelion strode out the door, walked down the steps and lit up on the patio.

"You need to watch your tone. You want her running off again?" Gladys said.

"I've got an office to run. I can't have my daughter burning her bra at the reception desk."

"It's just young people lingo," Gladys said.

"It's doper speak and it makes her sound stupid." Walter folded his paper and set it on the table. He stood up and finished his coffee. "I just want this to work out. Not just for me or her, but-," Walter nudged his head towards me.

"I know," Gladys said, "have a good day."

"So long," Walter said.

Gladys and I peeked out the window as Walter and Dandelion walked out to the car together.

"She'll make a pretty secretary," I said.

"Yes, she will. Did you see her this morning? Did you see her in that dress? She acted like she didn't like it, but I could tell she was happy about it. Her eyes gave her away. She was smiling on the inside."

I wanted to ask what that meant, smiling on the inside. Though I had never heard the phrase before, I kind of knew its meaning. I saw it on Dandelion too. She did look like she might be happy.

"Finish your cereal," Gladys said. I walked back over and sat down in front of my bowl. There was a dramatic difference in the way my cereal looked as opposed to the way it was photographed on the box. In the picture, the cereal was three times the size and was a beautiful looking crunchy brown. In my bowl, the flakes had turned into a gray gruel.

"Delicious every time," the slogan announced. I put a soggy spoonful in my mouth. Things were rarely what they seemed.

10

I didn't have much to move out, some boxes of clothes and toys and that was it. Walter helped us move into a small trailer on the west side of town. The trailer park was next to a lumber yard and some railroad tracks.

"Fun places to explore and ride your bike," Dandelion said. Even at the young age of eight I could tell it was a considerable step down, but Dandelion had insisted that Walter and Gladys not help her out. "I need to focus on getting better and to work for my own things," she told them. And for a while she did. She'd go to work every morning, cook a meal or a frozen pizza at night and then watch TV or play a board game with me. We'd see movies, go roller skating or to the park, but I could tell Dandelion was getting anxious. She told me she was lonely and that she needed some excitement in her life. She had a few dates with a guy from Walter's office and another one with some guy that taught shop at the high school, but not with anyone she was really crazy about.

She was having problems with Walter's authority at work. One day after an argument, she quit. A few days later she took a job as a cashier at the Food Fair grocery store. Her new job was for less money and more hours. She was always tired and started smoking in the trailer.

Men noticed Dandelion wherever we went. She smiled, flipped her hair, and flirted. Guys always asked for her phone number and she rarely turned anyone down. With Dandelion staying out later on her dates, I gained some new responsibilities. One was cooking dinner on the gas stove, which mostly consisted of beef stew or canned spaghetti. The other thing I learned was how to lock up at night when Dandelion called to say she wouldn't be home. Most kids my age would have been scared being left alone, hearing the arguments in the surrounding trailers, dogs barking, drunks laughing, but I was more concerned with Dandelion. I prayed every night that she would be okay. Living by the railroad tracks bothered most folks, but I found it soothing. Having that train roll through our troubled neighborhood was a symbol of normalcy. It was a reminder that in spite of all the drama that unfolded in our small trailer park, life for other people cruised on as scheduled.

One morning I awoke to the smell of fresh cinnamon rolls baking in the oven. I got up and went into the tiny kitchen of our trailer to find Dandelion smiling over a hot cup of coffee.

"Morning, kiddo," she said. She told me she had met somebody, someone who was smart and funny, a hard worker who made her happy. She said she had never felt better and she owed it all to the new man in her life, Randy. Moments later a dark-haired, barrel-chested man in his late thirties with a bushy moustache and an impressive collection of tattoos walked out of the bedroom in his underwear. He smelled like raw sewage.

"You must be Dork." He extended his hand.

"It's Roarke." I was cautious to stick out my hand, but I wanted to be polite. Just as we were about to shake Randy jerked his hand back and ran his fingers through his greasy hair.

"You wish," he said laughing.

I looked over at Dandelion. She sipped her coffee and smiled at me. "You guys will be great together."

Randy Pierson was a mechanic for the Southern Illinois Bus Company and though Dandelion had only been seeing him for a few weeks, he took it upon himself to move in on their one month anniversary.

Walter and Gladys couldn't stand Randy. "We should have named her Charmin the way she takes to assholes," Walter said. They were disgusted that Dandelion had allowed a known felon to move in with us, but Dandelion said it was her payments, her trailer, her life, and though they wanted to argue, they were just happy to have their little girl in town. At first it seemed as though we would all play our roles just fine. Randy would teach me about motors, Dandelion would be happy, but like the smell of a new car, it faded quickly.

Randy, or "Big Chief Nasty Ass" as he called himself, was either super happy or way down in the dumps. When he and Dandelion weren't "rasslin' nekkid" in the north end of the trailer they were making all out war all over the trailer park. They'd yell, fight, cuss, kick and scratch. Sometimes Randy would haul off and hit her. I'd step in only to get thrown to the side. Every time I tried to talk to Dandelion about it she would say that everything was okay. "Don't worry about it. We're just passionate people."

Sunday mornings, Walter and Gladys would pick me up for church. They would ask questions, want to know everything that was going on, but I never said a word. Walter didn't yell and Gladys didn't cry when they didn't know everything that was going on. Sometimes silence with a smile seemed to be the best way to handle things and keep the peace.

Sundays were Randy's "recovery days." He'd just sit on the couch in his underwear, chain smoke, and watch TV. On the way out the door to church one morning, Randy stopped me to give me a glimpse into the depth of his theological understanding.

"Don't just go praying for yourself now. We all got things we need so be sure to say some prayers for me too. And pray for something good. I wouldn't mind a raise."

It was clear to me Randy had never been to church before. A week earlier I had learned that people weren't supposed to ask for things for themselves when they prayed.

"Jesus does not work at Western Auto," my Sunday school teacher, Mrs. Taylor said. This was after I tossed in a brief request for a new bike while closing the classroom prayer. I was just a kid and if God wasn't going to give me a bike, a jerk like Randy certainly wasn't going to get a raise.

One day after Sunday service I was sitting at Donna's Cafe with Gladys and Walter. "If God is so great and loves us so much, why does he let bad things happen?" I asked.

Gladys deferred the question by looking to Walter. She was counting on him to provide a deep answer. Walter chewed his chicken fried steak thoughtfully then took a sip of his iced tea and swallowed. "God is busy, Roarke."

"Doing what?" I asked.

"Well, judging from recent sporting events and awards shows he is helping a lot of people win stuff."

"What about innocent people that drown in floods or are killed by volcanoes? Is he too busy to help them?"

"Only a moron would live by a volcano," Walter said.

"But God makes volcanoes."

"Nope. The devil makes those." Walter went right back to his meal.

"Honestly, Walter," Gladys said.

"Well, what do you want me to do, Gladys? Send the kid to Bible college?"

Gladys took a deep breath, "God gives us free will, and with that free will human beings sometimes invite things or people into their lives that they shouldn't."

"What do you mean?" I said.

"She means if people are stupid, do stupid things, then bad things can happen to them."

"Why do bad things happen to good people then? People that do the right thing?"

"Well, then that is what we call the shits," Walter said.

"How come you get to swear and I can't?"

"Because I fought in a war."

"So?" I said.

"It was the shits," Walter said.

Gladys let out a sigh. "Anyway, the devil doesn't make volcanoes or cause floods. That's nature."

"Hell's pretty hot though. Makes sense to me that the devil could make the volcanoes," Walter said, winking at me.

Gladys shook her head. "Honestly."

Later that day they drove me back to the trailer. "Remember what we said about stupid people today?" Walter said.

"Yeah."

"Well it doesn't get any better than that." Walter pointed at Randy who was bent under the hood of his truck pounding on something with a hammer. We both laughed until I had to get out of the car. Then I began to feel sick.

11

"Everybody loves partying over at Randy and Dandy's place," Randy crowed. He'd always barge in the front door carrying brown bags from the liquor store. The more he and Dandelion entertained at the trailer, the worse things got. Their friends began staying over later and partying longer. They'd eat all of our food and leave the mess behind. I'd find complete strangers passed out in my bed and once or twice caught Randy and Dandelion doing lines and having sex in the front room. "It's just powdered sugar, kid. Makes your mom sweeter," Randy laughed.

I wanted to go to the police, tell Gladys or Walter, but I didn't want Dandelion to get in trouble. I knew she was sick and needed help, but I didn't know what to do. Whenever I complained about Randy she would only get mad. The violence started to get worse too.

"Who in the hell scratched my *Nazareth* album? I know it wasn't me." Randy's friends always left the living room looking like a dumpster. His records would be scattered all over the floor, lying out of their dust jackets with all kinds of bottle caps and cigarette butts mixed among them. He'd smack me around for every scratch, even though I never touched them. I came to hate every artist featured on every album he owned. Whenever I heard *Jethro Tull* and saw the booze come out, I knew that there would be hell to pay the next day. I hated Randy. I could tell that sometimes Dandelion did too, but even after he'd hit her and she'd kick him out, she'd take the bastard back a few days later.

I loathed that trailer. On nights I didn't stay with Walter and Gladys I would leave for school as early as I could and stay as late as the teachers would let me. I'd shoot baskets on the playground, draw on the school steps, anything.

As much as I wanted to be away from Randy I needed to keep an eye on Dandelion. I decided I needed a lookout point. There was an apple tree in the back of the trailer park and from the top of its branches I could see our trailer. I grabbed a few small boards I found in the neighboring lumber yard's dumpster and nailed them together high up in the tree. I'd sit up there most nights Randy was around. Most of the time I drew in a notepad, sketching scenes from the trailer park. I sketched King, the mangy German shepherd that was chained to the step railing of trailer number seven. I drew the little squirts that played in the deep mud puddles left by the mobile home company's big rigs. I was amazed at the mix of laughter and tears that escaped all those tin walls. I drew nearly everyone that lived in our small tribe on the outskirts of town. Drew them, wadded them up then threw them away.

12

One Friday, Randy decided to call in sick and have a fish fry. The Bluegill & Bud Bash he called it. Nearly every loser and half-wit in town showed up to tie one on and cut loose. By the time I got home from school the party was in full swing. The trailer was packed with people dancing and groping one another to the sounds of *Black Oak Arkansas*. I tried to get in my room, but the door was locked. I tossed my book bag in a corner of the kitchen then went outside. Randy was standing over a huge pot of boiling oil he had sitting atop the blue flames of a camping stove. I went to grab a piece of fish that was cooling on paper towels only to have my hand knocked away by Randy's greasy tongs.

"Beat it, Roarke! That is for our guests."

"So what? That guy over there with the beard just ate one of my pudding cups."

Randy wrinkled his face up in a mocking fashion, "So, that guy over there just brought two cases of beer. What'd you bring?"

"I don't have to bring anything you asshole. You live in me and my mom's trailer."

Randy dipped his tongs in the boiling hot oil then flicked some on me.

"Oww, dick!"

"Don't stand so close to the fire, kid," Randy said, laughing.

I looked at his greasy clothes and tried to find something to make fun of. I spied one of his tattoos. It was a picture of a hand giving the finger on his forearm. It looked like a kindergartner had drawn it. I had meant to ask him about it before, but now with a crowd of his friends around it was the perfect time.

"What is that tattoo on your arm?"
"Which one?" Randy said.
"That one," I pointed.
"I got that in the joint. It's the bird. Know what it means?" He took a long swig of beer then burped. "Fuck off." A guy with a bandana on his head and a long pony tail stepped up and grabbed a piece of fish.
"I know what it means," I said. "I just didn't know that there were five-year-old tattoo artists in prison."
"BlaHaHaHahaaa!" Bandana laughed. He waved over another guy. "Hey Pete, doesn't Randy's tattoo look like a kid drew it?"
Pete walked over and laughed, "Holy shit! It does."
"A blind one," I said. There was more laughter. I was smiling at my new found comedy fans when Randy cuffed me in my right ear with his left hand.
I stumbled back and fell on my ass. My head was ringing.
"What else you got, smart ass?
"Jesus, Randy," Bandana said.
I held my ear and looked around. Everything seemed crooked. I was slow to get up. "I'm telling mom."
Randy looked at me and smiled. "What do you think is more important to her, living with a little prick like you or feeling a big prick like mine?" Randy grabbed his balls and gave a hearty tug.
I looked at the cooked fish cooling and decided I didn't want anything the man ever touched again. A woman with yellow hair and a leather vest walked up to Randy. She had a cigarette in one hand and a beer in the other. She leaned in close and rubbed herself against him. "You get done cooking fish, maybe you'd like to eat some clam?"
Randy pulled her to him and gave her a kiss. "Watch that around here," he said laughing. I cleared my throat, hacked up a big loogey then let it fly down on the fish. Randy swung his hot greasy tongs at me, but I ducked and took off running.
"You better not come back here tonight boy or I will kick your ass."

I was thirty yards away when I turned around. A handful of partiers that were outside looked at me. "When I tell Dandelion what you just did you'll be out of the trailer."

"Whooaaaa," the small group said around Randy in unison.

Randy took a hit off his beer. "She won't do shit," he said. He held up a small clear baggie of white powder. "I got the icing for her cake." Everyone laughed. I bent over and picked up a rock. I rotated it in my hand and thought about throwing it.

"Don't do it, boy," he said. "I'll kill you."

I kept my arm cocked back for a moment then brought it down and tossed the rock in the dirt. As full of shit as Randy was I knew he wasn't lying that time. Someone made the *bawk-bawking* sound of a chicken. There was more laughter. I turned and ran off to my tree praying for fire, flood, or a tornado to kill them all.

13

It was rare that I ever found any peace in that trailer, but occasionally I'd get it all to myself. Randy would either be working or "out on a run," and Dandelion would be at Food Fair ringing up people's groceries. I was sitting on the couch watching cartoons one day when there was a knock on the door. It was unusual as most people always barged in. If Gladys or Walter were coming over they always called first. I got up and opened the door. A chubby kid with red hair and freckles stood in front of me wearing a faded Chewbacca t-shirt. He looked to be about my age and was squinting from the sun.

"Hi. My name is Clem."

"I'm Roarke."

"My dad just moved over across the way." He pointed at number five, a beat up brown trailer. An older woman had lived there forever.

"Your dad bought old brownie?"

"No, my grandma left it to him in her will. She left me some money too. I got this bike." Clem pointed over at a brand new Hawk Five BMX bike.

"Cool!" I said.

"I thought maybe you could show me where you ride yours." He pointed at my bike leaning against the wall, a scratched up and rusted Huffy without a seat.

"Maybe later," I said. The last thing I wanted to do was ride bikes with some strange kid bragging about his new wheels and showing off. Besides, I knew *Wonder Woman* would be on soon. I didn't know it then, but I was slowly falling in love with Lynda Carter.

"You can ride my bike," Clem said. The kid looked lonely, a little uneasy.

"For how long?" I asked.

"As long as you want."

The chances of me ever actually meeting Wonder Woman were slim to none. The chances of her actually falling in love with me were even worse.

"Okay," I said. "I'll show you some good spots to ride."

"Thanks." He walked over and grabbed my bike.

The sport grips on his handlebars hugged my hands. Checked crash pads decorated and protected nearly every bar. The chrome stunt pegs on the back wheels shone like floodlights. It was an awesome bike. The kind of bike a kid could ride all the way across the country, or practice doing stunts on every day.

"Man, if I had a bike like this I would be the next Evel Knievel."

"Yeah well, please don't wreck it."

"I won't." I said. "Just yell if you can't keep up."

"How do you ride this thing without a seat?"

"Just don't sit down."

I squeezed both grips and brought my left foot down hard on the pedals. The bike took off like a rocket. I pumped the bike side to side and pushed my feet around in lightning quick circles. I jumped the railroad tracks then bunny hopped a rotting tree stump. I zigged and zagged through the tall weeds of the dusty worn pathways then cut through the lumber yard. Clem was about twenty yards behind me trying to acclimate to my clunker.

We rode through the cool shade of some tall trees then cut over to the park. From there we hit an empty soccer field, slid under an old fence and then rode out to the salt flats behind it. I took every jump I saw. Flying and soaring through the air felt amazing on such a smooth, well-built bike. The sun shone down as I pedaled around the makeshift track. Midway around a rusted out tractor near the back of a sloped bank, I suddenly remembered some older kids at school talking about feral dogs that lived back there. It had been forever since I had ridden back to the salt flats, but as I swung around the corner on the trail I heard the barking.

"What's that?" Clem asked.

"Go! Go! Go!" Four hungry dogs of varying sizes and mixed breeds rose up behind us. We both pedaled like our lives depended on it. "Follow me," I yelled. I was off and down the trail.

"Don't leave me!" Clem screamed. I pedaled back to where he was.

"Switch bikes," I yelled. Clem hopped off mine and I handed him his. He took off pedaling and I stayed right behind him.

"Tell me where to go."

"Go through those woods up there. There's a deep creek."

We both turned at the same time, blasting through the trees while the dogs barked behind us. The creek appeared before us as we got closer, but it was dry. I shot down one side and pedaled up the other as far as I could go then left my bike and scrambled on up the bank. Five feet away was an old barbed wire fence with new electric fence wires running across it. I dove under it head first like Pete Rose. Behind me, Clem rolled clumsily down the far bank then made it two feet up the other side.

"I can't leave my bike," he screamed. He was struggling, trying to pull his shiny new ride up the dry dirt wall. The dogs were five feet from the creek bed.

I crawled back under the fence and caught a jolt of electricity on my back. My adrenaline was pumping. I hopped up and saw the dogs running down the bank towards Clem. I grabbed a fallen branch and within seconds found myself in the bottom of the creek bed swinging it like Thor's hammer. I connected with fur and bone, kicking and screaming. I heard a whimper then swung again and got a brown one in the head. Two, three, four more swings connected. Three hounds were in retreat while the last one, a large black mutt, was barking with foamed jaws about to pounce. I looked down at the stick I was holding. It had broken in two. A large rock was two feet behind me. I turned to make a grab for it then heard a scream like I had never heard before. Out of my peripheral vision I saw

Clem's bike fly through the air and land on the charging dog. I heard something pop and a whimpering howl. The beast scrambled out from beneath the bike and took off limping away.

I looked over at Clem. His eyes were as big as saucers and tears rolled down his dusty cheeks. My temples were pulsing and I realized I had tears in my eyes too. I felt like my heart was going to beat out of my chest. I tried to catch my breath. Clem went over to pick up his bike. It looked fine except for a slightly bent back stunt peg that had black bloody fur on the end of it.

"You saved my life," I said.

"You're bleeding."

I looked at my arm. Two claw marks were a dark red and the third was oozing blood. I took my t-shirt off and wrapped it around my arm. "Did they get you?"

"No," Clem said, bending over catching his breath.

"How did you pick up your bike like that?"

"Dunno," Clem said, "I just did it."

I went up and grabbed my Huffy. "Too bad you didn't throw my bike. You might have done it some good." We both started laughing, then laughed harder. It was more about release than humor. "Let's get out of here before they come back."

We rode all away around the fence, back to the road then on across the soccer field. "What grade are you in?" I asked.

"Fifth. What about you?"

"Same. Are you going to go to school here?"

"I don't know. My parents are divorced. Right now I'm just visiting."

As we got closer to the trailer park I could hear Randy's music playing. There was no telling who he had with him or what he would be doing. Clem and I both turned the corner and saw him in the distance with his head underneath the hood of his truck.

"Is that your dad?" Clem said.

"Hell no," I said. "That's my mom's boyfriend."

"Is he a mechanic?"

"No. Just a dick."

Clem laughed. "Don't you get in trouble for cussing?"

"No. I fought in a war. Is your dad going to be mad about your bike?"

"I'll just tell him I wrecked it. He'll be home from work soon and fix it."

"I'd get clobbered."

"Really?"

"Actually, Randy wouldn't even care," I said. And that felt worse.

"Hey, I might be back next week or so. What else do you do around here?"

"Draw up in that tree sometimes. Play at the park."

"Do you have a fort?"

"No. Just a couple of old boards nailed together."

"Maybe when I come back we can build a fort."

"Maybe."

"I gotta go," Clem said.

"See you later." I turned my bike and gave it one hard down pedal. I coasted over to our trailer and watched Randy. He tapped his foot to his music and looked over the engine with a cigarette dangling from his mouth.

"Well look what the cat dragged in," he said. I held the t-shirt tight to my arm.

"Do you know what time Dandelion gets home tonight?"

"Seven or so." Randy looked at the bloody t-shirt and didn't say a word.

I swung my bike around and pedaled off in the other direction.

14

I liked school. School was an opportunity to be out of the house. I sat at my desk looking at the math quiz in front of me. I wasn't prepared for it, but I didn't care. It was just a piece of paper with some numbers on it. It was nothing to run or hide from. It couldn't hit or hurt me. I rolled down the problems as fast as I could. Everything was a race as a kid. Who ran the fastest, who drank their milk the fastest. Within one minute I had answered all twenty-five questions. I turned my paper over to show that I was finished then put my head down as though I were weary with boredom from the simple problems.

Up near the front of the room George Bentley worked away. Normally he finished first. He always made a big production of pulling a book out of his desk and pretending to thoughtfully read while the rest of us were barely down the middle of the page.

I let out a small fake cough. George turned around to look at me, stunned that I had finished before him. I smiled smugly. His coordinated outfit was neatly pressed and his hair was combed perfectly and sprayed in place. He shook his head and turned back to work. I leaned back in my chair, pleased, and cracked my knuckles. Who cared if all his answers were right and mine were wrong? For one day, I, Roarke Davenport, had finished victorious. I huffed on my nails and rubbed them on my shirt. A few students looked over at me and scowled.

I looked across the back of the room. A fat kid named Stewart was bent over his paper sobbing and erasing his answers. His navy blue Dallas Cowboys sweatshirt barely covered his round stomach and snot marks were streaked across his sleeve from where he had wiped his runny nose. I couldn't believe it, tears over times tables? Surely his head would explode when we got to long division.

Stewart's parents were wealthy overachievers. His mother was a judge in town and his father was a retired fiddle player, or as Stewart was always quick to point out, a concert violinist. No idea how they ended up in Briarfield.

The teachers always kept a close eye on Stewart. It was no secret in school that the kid had some problems. Stewart had told a school counselor earlier that year that he wanted to kill himself because he couldn't figure out how to ride his bike. He told his parents it had been stolen, but some kids later found it by the old rusted trestle bridge.

I felt bad for the kid in a way, but he was soft. His folks dropped him off at school in a nice car, he never rode the bus, his mom packed his lunch for him, and he always had a brand new pair of Nikes. How school could save one kid and terrify another was beyond me. Later Stewart would be at home enjoying an ice cream sundae, watching *Zoom*, and I'd be up hiding in my poorly self-built tree house while Dandelion and Randy had their friends over. It was strange how things panned out like that.

Half the class was still slumped over their quizzes. I picked up my pencil and started drawing on the back of my paper. Drawing was my saving grace. A tablet of paper and a pencil allowed me to escape from whatever I was dealing with at home. I drew a picture of Stewart holding his head, running and screaming from a gigantic 2x2=. I shaded in his clothes, picked up on his features, and accentuated the picture with action marks. The number twos in the picture both had bloodshot eyes and nasty open mouths with slime dripping off their razor sharp teeth. Underneath the picture I wrote the caption "Math Problems." I heard a snicker come from behind the seat next to me. I turned and saw Lisa Perrimore smiling. I smiled back and lifted my drawing up so she could get a better look at it. This time she laughed out loud.

I loved Lisa Perrimore. I imagined when I got older, found a job, and made some money that I would buy a big wooden sailboat and we would sail away together. When I wasn't busy navigating dangerous swells and fighting pirates, I would fish and cook meals for us. We'd hold hands and sip wine while we sailed into the sunset.

"Mr. Davenport, would you please care to tell me what it is that makes you so special?" It was my teacher, Marilyn Lutz. She was pretty except for a huge hairy mole on her cheek. I turned around quickly.

"What?"

"Bring your paper up here this minute." Ms. Lutz rivaled Genghis Khan in her lack of mercy and it was all because of her mole. We all made fun of her for it behind her back. Occasionally, me or some other brave kid would scream out "Holy Moly" on a dare. Sometimes we'd get spanked. Sometimes she would just walk out of the room. Some teachers wanted their students to be smart. Ms. Lutz was the other kind. She reveled in her students stupidity. I walked up and handed her my paper. She eyed my work then smiled. "All of these are wrong."

George looked up from his quiz grinning. Stewart still wept in the background like an injured dog. Ms. Lutz turned my paper over and looked at the drawing.

"What's this?"

"I was joking around," I said.

"You think it's funny that Stewart is having a hard time?"

"Not really."

"You'll be lucky to cut Stewart's lawn someday. You know that?"

"Let's just hope he can figure out what to charge me," I said. Chuck Peterson let out a small chuckle.

"Take your F and artwork with you to the principal's office. I'll be down there with my paddle shortly." The room fell silent. Stewart stopped crying and even George looked a little scared for me. I looked out over the rest of the room. Lisa kept her head down looking at her quiz. Her knight was being sent to the gallows and she couldn't even wave goodbye. My false victory had been short lived.

"Go now, Roarke," Ms. Lutz said. I turned and walked out the door. Down the hall a bit I looked at my paper and smiled. It was a hell of a drawing.

15

We rarely ever sat down to eat at the table together, but since Principal Whitman had called Dandelion to remark about the detail of my drawing, she thought it was a special occasion. Dandelion made a box of Hamburger Helper. Even Randy, Big Chief Nasty Ass himself was sitting at the table.

"Gifted? That's what they're calling it now? When I was a kid they called it being a pussy." Randy ate his food like a caveman. He hung over his plate as though he were in a race. His fork stuck out of his fist like a scoop shovel.

"Not hardly," Dandelion said. "His teachers say he has real talent, an eye for picking things up. Not your standard stick figure bullshit. Right, Roarke?"

"I guess so." I had to eat fast. Randy was closing in on his third plate of food and I had to be quick if I wanted seconds.

"Hell, I thought gifted was what you called somebody with a twelve inch pecker," Randy said laughing. Dandelion lit a cigarette and blew a plume of smoke over the table.

"Well, I think it's terrific," Dandelion said. Randy tossed his fork down on his empty plate.

"Alright, by God, let's see this great drawing. I imagine you'll have it in a frame before too long." Dandelion looked at me and smiled.

"Should we show him?"

"I don't care." I wiped my mouth with a paper towel.

"Hell yeah! Show me! Let's see it. Let's see the great Roarke drawing."

Dandelion got up with her cigarette and walked back to my room. She walked out seconds later holding my drawing and handed it to Randy. I wanted to see his reaction. I wanted to see him bow to my greatness. I wanted him to say he was sorry for being such an asshole and ask me for forgiveness. Randy looked at it for a moment silently and took a swig of his beer.

"What the hell is this? Some kid running from numbers? I don't get it." Randy was mad at me. I had told Dandelion earlier about the woman he kissed at the fish fry. She had asked him about it, but he was quickly forgiven.

"Look at the title," Dandelion said. "Math problems. Pretty funny."

"Shit," Randy said, "go get me your drawing paper."

"Seriously?"

"You two want to see a drawing? I'll show you how it's done." Dandelion gave me a funny look. I got up and got my tablet out of my room, walked back and handed it to Randy.

"I didn't know you could draw, baby," Dandelion said to Randy.

"Shit yeah, I can. I'll show you a picture."

Dandelion cleared our paper plates. I watched Randy try to draw. For the next hour and a half Randy sat at the kitchen table drinking beer, cussing under his breath, erasing time and time again, before tearing out a page in my tablet and starting over. Occasionally, he'd blame the supplies for his artistic inadequacies, "this pencil sucks," or "this paper is shit," he'd say. Finally, he finished and put his pencil down.

"Try this on for size." Randy handed us his masterpiece and proudly drained another can of beer. His drawing was hard to make out with all the ripped and torn paper where he had violently erased. It looked like a toddler had scribbled it with his toes. It looked like a car of some kind.

"How you like them apples?" He sniffed. "Gifted my ass. Guess we have two artists in the house now."

"What is it?" Dandelion asked.

"That is a supercharged Pontiac GTO, darlin'."

"Sure did erase a bunch," I said.

"You sure did," Dandelion said. We both looked at one another and smiled.

"Well?" Randy sat proudly with his arms crossed.

"Don't quit your day job," Dandelion said to Randy. We both burst out laughing. Dandelion laughed so hard she nearly wet her pants. Milk shot out of my nose. I felt a sharp sting on my left cheek and fell back in my chair. I saw the table legs rise up from the ground and flip over onto Dandelion. The screen door slammed. I crawled over to her. "I'm okay," she said. "Are you alright?"

"I'm okay."

We both got to our feet and lifted the table back up on its legs. I picked my picture up off the floor. It was wet from spilled milk. I wadded it up and tossed it in the trash.

Dandelion dusted herself off and saw Randy's picture under a chair. She grabbed a pen from the counter and wrote "Nice Job!" in the upper left hand corner then walked over and stuck it to the fridge with a magnet. We both looked at it and started laughing again. Not caring if he could hear us or not.

16

Weeks went by and Dandelion was dropping a lot of weight. Her face looked tired and gaunt and she rarely ate. Randy had gotten fired from the bus company. There were more fights and abuse. I got to be quick, learned how to duck and dive, absorb a blow, lie still on the ground. Mom did too, but she found something else to dull the pain. Drugs became a daily part of her routine again.

"I'd like you two to meet Larry and Bernard," Randy said, his arm extended out to two guys that looked like they crawled out from under a rock. Larry had a scar that ran under his left eye and his black hair was matted like a stray dog. Bernard was short and fat. He had the words "love" and "hate" tattooed on his knuckles. "Larry and Bernard will be staying with us for awhile, so if they need anything you two help them out." Dandelion asked to speak to Randy in the back. He excused himself and closed the door behind them. I heard mom say something. It was met with a cold smack.

Larry and Bernard laughed. "Here we go," Larry said. I tried to run to the back of the trailer to help Dandelion, but Bernard tripped me.

"Mind your own business, kid."

Dandelion sent me over to Walter and Gladys' more, but with special instructions not to tell them a thing. I wanted to, but she made me promise. She said she could go to jail too.

The neighbors called the police over to the trailer a few times, but they never had a warrant. They arrested Randy twice for being drunk and disorderly, and took Dandelion down once too. Larry and Bernard would sit in the trailer smoking, playing Atari, and then go bail Randy out. Although the police suspected illegal activity they couldn't prove anything illegal was going on. I'd snoop around whenever I had the chance, but I couldn't find where Randy hid their drugs.

On nights I didn't stay with Walter and Gladys I would sit up in my tree drawing for hours by flashlight. I would brace my body against the branches and boards so that I could fall asleep safely. One night I woke up from the cold and looked down on the trailer. All of the lights were out and everything was quiet. I climbed down out of the tree and walked back home. The door was unlocked as usual. Randy's clothes were thrown on the couch. I could hear him snoring in the back room.

I opened the door to my bedroom and kicked off my shoes. My eyes adjusted to the darkness. With the moonlight from the window it looked as though someone was in my bed.

"Roarke? Is that you?" Dandelion rose up. "You okay, honey?"

"Yeah. Did he hit you? Are you hurt?"

"I'm fine," she said. She got out of my bed. "I just wanted to lay here until you came home. I love you, you know."

"I know."

Dandelion kissed me. "Go to sleep."

I tossed my stuff on the dresser and took my shirt off. I looked after her as she walked out of my bedroom on down the hall. Moonlight from a window splintered the shadows and I could see she was carrying a knife. I heard a drawer in the kitchen open and close.

I put on a pair of athletic shorts and walked out to the living room. Dandelion was lying on the couch.

"What happened?"

"Nothing. Just a little fight."

"Let's leave this loser."

"I can't, Roarke." She looked like she hadn't slept in weeks.

"Go sleep in my room, okay. I forgot I need to read some books for school."

"Yeah," Dandelion said. "You sure?"

"Of course."

Dandelion padded off to my room. I looked down at the coffee table and spied an old barkeeper's tool lying amidst a number of bottle caps and a full ashtray. I picked it up and squeezed it until the curled metal prong poked out between my middle and index finger. If Randy came out mean in the morning I'd be ready. I stretched out on the couch facing Randy and Dandelion's bedroom. A late night rerun of *The Brady Bunch* was on TV. What a bunch of milquetoasts. I watched as much as I could bear then dozed off.

I woke up around seven. Everyone was still asleep. I got up, dressed, and grabbed a Twinkie for breakfast on my way out. Halfway across the gravel lot I turned around and ran back to the trailer. I peeked in my room at Dandelion. She was sleeping soundly. I kissed her on the cheek.

17

At Dandelion's urging I had been staying over at Walter and Gladys's place for a few weeks. Dandelion sold it that she was working odd hours and that Randy had found some work out of town. "Sounds like a scoop of horseshit to me," Walter said.

"Maybe they just need some space and time to work things out," Gladys said.

"Work what out? That he's an asshole? She needs to kick that loser to the curb. Right, Roarke?"

"Right," I said.

Sometimes at night I'd pedal my bike over to their trailer to see if they were there. I felt bad not believing Dandelion, but I was worried after that night I found her in my bedroom. Every time I rode out there, no lights were on. I didn't hear Randy's music blaring. Maybe my mom was telling the truth.

I was at school when they came to tell me that Randy and Dandelion were dead. Ms. Lutz and Principal Whitman talked to the police for awhile then called me over. Some kids whispered to one another while others stayed quiet. They had seen the cops come find me before, but this time it seemed different. Their looks were no longer of annoyance, but of deep concern. There had been an accident, an explosion that morning.

Sometime after nine Bernard evidently had stopped by to see Randy at the trailer. When he got there all the doors and windows were closed which was strange because the trailer didn't have air conditioning. The trailer was locked, so Bernard used a key Randy had given him. He had only been in the door two seconds before the cherry of his cigarette had ignited the gas. For an explosion of that size firemen guessed the stove had been left on for more than eight hours. Other than a few second degree burns the explosion had thrown Bernard clear of the accident. Dandelion and Randy weren't so lucky. Both had died in what was a hellish and fiery blaze. It was ruled an accidental death, but later amidst the charred rubble they found some drug paraphernalia and cash. Some investigators believed Bernard had killed Randy and Dandelion over a drug deal. Others said it was just a plain stupid accident by people too doped up to use a stove properly.

A few days later somebody from the county came by to speak to Walter while the three of us were watching the sunset from the porch.

"Good afternoon, Mr. Davenport."

"Hello, Sam."

"I was hoping I could speak to you for a moment."

Walter looked at Gladys and me and nodded. We went inside the house. Gladys went to the kitchen to refill our lemonades. I stayed near the front of the house listening through the screen door.

"What's going on?"

"Mr. Pierson, it appears, has no next of kin willing to claim his remains. I didn't know if –"

"Roarke!" Walter called. I froze. He knew I was there. "Come out here."

I waited a moment or two then walked out, "Yeah?"

"Sam here is telling me that Randy didn't have any family. Wants to know if we want to pay to bury his remains? Thoughts on that?"

"No. I mean I-"

"Sam, surely there is a farmer around here that has an old outhouse pit that needs to be capped. Drop that gigantic turd down there."

"I understand," Sam said. He shook Walter's hand and walked away.

"Have your grandmother come back out here will ya?"

I turned around and Gladys was already on her way. She handed each of us our glasses and sat back down on the porch swing next to Walter. I had a seat on the steps.

"Everything okay, dear?" Gladys asked.
"Okay," Walter said.

Gladys and Walter took me to a shrink who told me it wasn't my fault, but I still felt like I should have been there. I would have noticed that the windows weren't open. I rode by the burnt out shell on my bike every few days and spoke to Dandelion. I told her how sorry I was, how much I missed her. How pissed I was she let such an asshole live with us. I'd sometimes sit in the apple tree and sketch the smoldered wreckage or what the trailer must have looked like while it was on fire. Then one day they hauled it away.

Dandelion was buried on the family plot just east of town. Her headstone read *Amanda Renae Davenport, beloved daughter and mother (1957–1983)*. Against Walter's wishes Gladys had a dandelion etched onto the granite.

When I got older Walter told me he believed Dandelion had done it on purpose. "Amanda knew what she was doing. That gas killed them both before the fire. She was a drug addict. She knew it and she was ashamed. He fed her the poison that she couldn't say no to."

"I don't want to remember her that way," I said.

"Me either. That's what pictures and old movies are for. I'm sure you got a good memory or two locked away in your heart somewhere. Something she may have said, a special day."

That was when I knew I wanted to be an artist. It was the one thing Dandelion saw me do well before she died. When I wasn't playing sports I had my head in a notebook, drawing and sketching. Someday my art would take me to far off places where people didn't know anything about me, only see my art and nod appreciatively.

18

I woke up in the living room of my small farmhouse. The portraits of Walter and Dandelion stared directly at me. They looked real. I missed them. In my tired hungover dream state I wondered if they could talk to one another from their easels. Had they spoken while I slept? Had they made up yet?

It was almost eight. I got up and started some coffee. I stood behind the kitchen sink looking out the back window. Ed Runyon, the man I rented the place from was far out in the fields already ambling along on his old tractor. The man manicured his land better than most folks took care of their own lawns. He was a tough old guy, an old friend of Walter's.

"There's the man that tames the land." Walter would say whenever he saw Ed. Walter always had odd sayings and funny quips he'd break out from time to time. One year Gladys won the quilting bee that was held between a few of the local churches. She purchased new fabrics and a sewing machine with her prize money. She asked Walter if he could clear out the small room in the back of the garage for her to set up shop. She thought it would be fun to have her friends over and possibly start her own little quilting business. Surely Walter would have been excited to see that his wife had aspirations beyond the ordinary.

"Everybody's got a sweet tooth, Gladys, but there is only so much taffy to go around."

Another time, before she ran away, Dandelion had asked Walter if he would drive her to Mt. Vernon to purchase some colored light up suspenders that she could wear to the skating rink. Walter replied with one of his favorites, "A show pony may win a blue ribbon or two, but it damn sure don't win many races. No one likes a show off, Amanda."

Walter had called me a show pony once. It was my first game in Little League with the pitching machine. The baseball field in the park had four rows of bleachers on each side. Dandelion and Walter weren't talking to each other for whatever reason that day and sat opposite one another on opposing baselines. Pitching machine league was for third and fourth graders. It was different from tee ball in that a mechanically powered white rubber wheel spun thirty miles an hour and hurled random balls and strikes over the plate. I could really smack the horse hide in tee ball, but I knew nothing about hitting a moving target. A pimply high school kid fed baseballs into the black abyss of the spinning wheel.

Kids were striking out left and right. Parents cheered and yelled in the stands. The team on the field chattered away. "Suh-wing battah, suh-wing!" I stood in the on deck circle waiting my turn, swinging my bat. I looked up to the sky and prayed for rain. The girl in front of me hit a triple on overthrows. Her parents were going ape shit and others were cheering. It was a hard act to follow.

Dust rose from the infield like steam. I spit as I walked up to home plate. My pulse quickened. Walter and Dandelion both hollered encouragement to me. It seemed odd, seeing as how neither of them had ever taken the time to pitch an actual baseball to me. They must have thought my coach would have me batting like a pro after just a few practices. All the other kids dads worked with them. Me? I just studied the likes of Willie McGee and Darrell Porter during Cardinals games.

I turned to look at Walter for any kind of instruction, but he was too busy arguing with Dandelion. "Nice to see you could finally make it to one of his games," he yelled across to Dandelion. I felt lonely standing there. For the first time I got the sense that if I ever did anything in life it was going to be on my own.

I was tired of being scared and unsure of things. I hated I didn't know how to bat well, but I wasn't going to let anyone in the crowd know. I pushed my batting helmet down on top of my head like the pros. I got in my stance and wiggled my bat like I'd been playing for years. The crowd noise quieted. Even the kids in the outfield stopped chattering and stepped a back a few paces. I could feel all eyes in the stands on me. I dug my front left foot into the dirt and waited. I stood there crowding the plate. The acne-scarred kid behind the pitching machine held the baseball up for me to see then slowly brought it down by the white spinning rubber wheel. "You ready?" he said. I nodded. The first pitch shot out of the machine. I pulled back then took a powerful swing.

"Strike one!"

I held up my arm and signaled for a time out. I stepped out of the batter's box and tapped the dirt from my cleats. I stretched for a moment then spit into the dirt. From the bleachers I heard Walter yell, "Hey, look at the show pony!" Everybody laughed. Dandelion yelled something to him and then he yelled back. Other parents and the coaches looked at both of them. I hung tough and pretended not to hear a thing. Two more balls and a strike followed.

"Watch the ball, Davenport!" Christine Bluthe yelled from the dugout. Her triple was a joke, but she had at least hit the ball. Her parents would no doubt offer to take the team out for pizza after the game. I didn't want to sit over a slice of pepperoni hearing about her triple then how I followed *a girl* and struck out. I couldn't bear it.

The next pitch came rifling out of the machine. It was headed right over the plate. I wanted to swing, but the fear of missing was too much. At the last minute I stepped into the ball's path and felt the horsehide sink deep into my arm with a dull thud. The crowd gasped. Any other kid would have cried, but I just stood there and acted like the badass that I wasn't.

"Are you okay, kid?" said the umpire.

"Yeah," I said spitting into the dirt like it was no big deal.

"Take your base," he said.

I tossed my bat to the side and headed down the dusty baseline. My arm throbbed and felt like it was swelling up underneath my uniform, but it didn't matter, I was on base. I spit in the dust again, pushed my helmet down, and took a nice lead off. I felt like a fraud.

I poured myself a cup of coffee, lit a cigarette, and walked out to the front porch. Grasshoppers leapt about the tall rows of corn. I was going to be showing some of my paintings the following day and I had some work to do. Other than the portraits of Walter and Dandelion, I had another painting I was working on and several more I had finished. The one I was most proud of was one where a man and woman were walking away from each other on a dark sidewalk. In between them was a glowing neon sign that said "Bar." I titled it *Placards for the Faint of Heart*. Two more titled, *She Said Tuesday*, and *Blue Rain*, were framed and ready to sell as well. I took a sip of coffee. Some dribbled down my sweater. I rubbed the drops off with my hand then looked at the four stubs where my fingers once were.

19

I was a junior in high school. I had Ellsworth breaking on the left and Simmons trailing behind him. Nelson filled the right lane. I dribbled to the top of the key, forcing Adams to commit then flipped the ball behind my back to Ellsworth for the lay-up. A whistle blew.

"Jesus Christ, Davenport, what in the hell was that?"

"That was an assist, coach." Some of the guys laughed.

"You trying to win a conference championship this year or impress all the pussy in the crowd?"

"You really want me to answer that?" More laughter.

"Run the lines. Mason you get in here for the hot shot. Fundamental basketball wins games."

Coach blew his whistle then pointed me to the sideline. I walked over and started running.

I wasn't the best player on the team, but I started. I enjoyed playing, but it wasn't a religion for me. Coach Barker told everyone that all he ever wanted was for his players to have fun, but he was full of shit. He read Ian Fleming novels and watched *Dallas,* and for that the guy considered himself to be an intellectual. The man actually had aspirations of coaching college hoops someday. He dressed like a second hand car salesman on game nights, mimicked Chuck Daly's moves on the sidelines, and chewed on an unlit cigar like Red Auerbach, yet had the nerve to call me a hot shot. He ran practice like a drill sergeant and blew his whistle the minute we started enjoying ourselves.

I had a decent jump shot, but it wasn't going to save the world. It did, however, have its benefits. The night I had twenty-three points against Red Hill, I lost my virginity to Mandy Wilson, a senior center on the girls basketball team.

Both junior varsity and varsity for both the girls and boys teams rode on the same bus for away games. Some players elected to ride with their parents, but the action on those long dark rides home had many clamoring for the prized back seats on the bus. That night boarding the bus, Mandy ran up and grabbed my hand.

"You're sitting next to me," she said. The two of us had talked briefly at a few parties, but nothing that led me to believe she liked me. It wasn't until the bus rolled out of town and the street lights went down on the highway that we started kissing. She unbuttoned her jacket and put my hand up her sweatshirt. She wasn't wearing a bra. We kissed for a few more minutes and then her head disappeared. Why anyone would want to ride home with their parents was beyond me.

It was a little after midnight on a Friday. Clem Burris, Toby Simmons and I were riding back from a barn party out near Mill Shoals. The music was blasting and we were passing a joint around. I was leaning back in the passenger seat, sipping a beer.

"You guys did it on the bus?" Clem asked.

"Not while it was moving. We snuck back on after it parked at the high school."

"Mandy Wilson," Toby said, "that is truly one tall drink of water."

"Great legs," Clem said. "Did you wear a rubber?"

"Yeah, she had one."

"What a whore!" Toby said.

"I prefer to think of her as a responsible gal that knows a well hung stud when she sees one." I said.

"Funny she hasn't fucked me then," Clem said, cracking a fresh beer.

"Her eyes are too close together," Toby said

"How are the eyes on the crusty washcloth beneath your bed?" I said. We all laughed.

I was holding my right hand straight out of the window moving it up and down in the air like little kids do. Suddenly from out of nowhere a doe jumped out into the middle of the road. Clem swerved to keep from hitting it and the car spun out on the gravel. Beers went flying everywhere. As we spun around my right hand hit the side of a low, bent metal road sign. I felt a pinch, kind of a sting. The car finally skidded to a stop. We sat there for a moment.

"You guys alright?" Clem asked.

"I'm good," Toby said, "you Roarke?"

"Turn the light on." I brought my hand into the car and examined it under the interior light. The sign had sliced off all four of my fingers just below the knuckle. I held my hand up above my lap, applying pressure. It didn't look like it belonged to me.

20

"You blew it," were Walter's words.

"That's enough," Gladys said, "It was a freak accident."

"What do you want me to do, Gladys? Give the kid a hug? Tell him we all make mistakes? Hell, he's right-handed and has no fingers. Sports are out the window, working a job anywhere is going to be tough, and forget about ever drawing again."

"I've always got soccer," I joked.

"Not goalie." Walter countered. He was always faster than me.

"People can overcome tragedies, dear. It happens every day."

"Yeah," Walter said. "Well, the worst kind of tragedies are the ones you bring on yourself. I guess the lesson in this is you're now officially old enough to fuck up on your own."

It was the only time in my life I had ever heard Walter drop an f-bomb. I looked at the bandage on my hand. I could hear the faucet drip. We all stood in the kitchen studying the linoleum floor.

"I got work to do in the garage," Walter said. Gladys and I watched him walk out the back door and down the brick path. His white thinning hair blew in the breeze.

"The doctor told him your BAC level was high and you had traces of marijuana in your blood." It was strange to hear Gladys say the words BAC and marijuana. "What are you doing, Roarke?"

21

A lot of people had mixed opinions about me not competing in athletics my senior year, but it wasn't the same. Some people called me a quitter. I viewed myself as a realist. That summer I spent the entire time working with my left hand, trying different prosthetic devices on my right, but nothing could come close to equaling the touch of my real fingers on the leather ball. I found the handicapped athletes on TV to be courageous and inspiring; skiing, running, and competing in triathlons in spite of their various disabilities, but for me, unless I could perform at the same level I didn't want to play. I was good with ten fingers, but I was marginal with six. I didn't want people to feel sorry for me, slouching off on defense, clapping because I caught a pass. I played in the park all through June and July. At night I tried to hold a pencil between my thumb and hand and draw, but it wasn't the same. When summer wound down before my senior year I decided to put my basketball and pencils away.

22

The funny thing is that it took me losing four fingers on my right hand to find my own unique artistic style. Prior to that I was good at drawing, but it was nothing unique. I mean I could draw things exactly as I saw them, but it wasn't extraordinary. There are hundreds of thousands of talented people out there that can draw. I was just another one. My painting was the same way, it was good, but that's all that it was. There was nothing fancy about it, no personal panache. My teachers told me I would be a terrific architect or draftsman. I could illustrate technical manuals or draw for trade publications, but there was no signature mode of expression in my work.

I remember painting *Iron Maiden* album covers on the back of some jean jackets for friends in high school. It was impressive work, but only to them. To anyone else it was an accurate copy, a good translation of an original work. I needed something special. I needed something new, but try as I might I couldn't find it.

I worked with chalk, ink, acrylics, oils, water colors, pencil, but my stuff was always just there, standard, good, but nothing earth shattering. As a right-handed person, the day I lost my fingers I lost every amount of skill I had in sports and drawing, work or otherwise. I tried painting with my left hand, training it to hold a brush, but the accuracy and touch just wasn't there. Even if it had been close, my paintings would have just gotten back to their standard look.

One day, Ms. Fowls, my art teacher suggested I try painting with my thumb. I laughed at the idea at first, but she kept telling me I should try it.

"Your hand had a keen ability to move when you held a pencil or brush. You still have your hand, just not your fingers. Use your thumb."

It was in her fourth period class one day when I finally tried it. I distinctly remember dipping my thumb in brown paint and touching the canvas. From that moment everything changed. My strokes were shorter, more sporadic. The paint went on thicker, more layered. The look of everything I did was drastically different. What would have been polished pictures became rough hewn, what looked to be average became extraordinary. Work that was stifled by a pursuit of perfection now was able to breathe and live in the new chaotic strokes of my damaged hand. I saw things differently, more realistically and by being able to see things more clearly I was able to paint them in a more complex and disorderly manner just like they were in real life. I painted all day and night. I tried new things constantly and pushed the boundaries and parameters of what I was being taught in art class.

"You are doing wonderful things here, Mr. Davenport." Ms. Fowls told me one day. "Maybe you'd like to do some painting here after school. Use our supplies, enjoy the quiet?"

"Cool."

"The one caveat is I want you to enter this year's high school art competition. It starts in the school district and then the winners move on from there."

"I'm not good enough to enter any kind of contest."

"Sure you are. You're a natural. I want to teach you all I know about art, but I want you to find your own way on the canvas."

"I guess I could do it after school. I don't have basketball practice anymore."

"You'll need to take it more seriously than you did basketball."

"I think I can handle that."

23

Within months I had studied numerous classic, modern and postmodern styles: impressionism, cubism, pop art, and surrealism. I used different paints, worked on different surfaces, tried multiple media and various techniques. I would move, push, smash, streak, and scratch the canvas with paint. I improvised like a jazz musician, added and experimented like a chef measuring ingredients with his eyes instead of with cups. The understanding of different types of painting made it easier to experiment and branch out. It was like my thumb had a mind of its own. Things I could only see in my head began appearing on the canvas.

I was developing an interesting style all my own. Thick, thin, tiny, big, blended and straight from the tube, my paintings were squiggles, lines and smears of color creating pictures of people, places and emotions I had known or someday hoped to. The confidence I had lost with my fingers I had rediscovered with my thumb. I no longer noticed my stumps when I looked at my right hand, but rather my future.

The contest came and I entered a 3' x 2' painting. It was of Dandelion and I sitting on the kitchen floor with the turned over table behind us just after Randy had gone on his rampage. I titled it *Critics*. It made it all the way to the state finals in Champaign before losing to a sophomore's oil painting of the White House lit up on a snowy Christmas night.

"Yours was better," Ms. Fowls said.

"His was pretty good. I couldn't do something like that."

"He can't do what you do. You made it to the finals on your first try."

"That's pretty cool I guess."

"Yes, it is. It's very cool."

I put my picture in her backseat and got in the front. Ms. Fowls' car was spotless on the interior. There was a little wear and tear, but it was pristine. It was natural for most people to clean their cars before they went on a trip with someone, but I got the feeling she kept it this way all the time. It felt lonely.

"Let's go celebrate your success."

"Okay," I said.

The Pie Shop was just outside Effingham and the place smelled like heaven. We got a small booth by a window and ordered coffee and two pieces of rhubarb pie.

"One of the judges mentioned how much depth your painting had. The subject matter. Is there a story behind it?"

"Yeah," I said. I told Ms. Fowls about the whole episode with my drawing and Randy. Mom and I laughing as he tried to one up me. The way he lost it and tore up the place. She listened intently. She knew how Dandelion died. Everyone in the teacher's lounge and town for that matter knew.

"I'm sorry for all of that," Ms. Fowls said.

"No big deal." I took a bite of pie.

"Life experiences definitely define who we are. Make us interesting."

"Yeah, I could have ended up painting something lame like the White House."

Ms. Fowls laughed. "I knew you thought yours was better."

"Not better, but the White House? I thought it was boring. Art is supposed to provoke thought, all that made me do was want to take a nap."

Ms. Fowls smiled, "You're learning. Technique is nothing if the subject isn't there."

I wanted to ask Ms. Fowls about her life. What brought her to Briarfield? Was she married? Did she have kids? But there was something that told me not to ask. She was a thin woman in her late sixties. She wore white blouses with gray wool skirts and kept her hair pulled back in a white ponytail.

"I want you to have my painting," I said.

"What?" She said. "No, you need that on your wall for inspiration. It's a special picture. Do you know how many artists you beat out?"

"Nah. You have it. You were the one that believed in me. Pushed me. No telling what I'd have done without you taking the time you did." I took a sip of coffee and when I looked up she was dabbing tears from her eyes.

"I don't know what to say. Thank you. I'll put it in my classroom. When kids ask me I can proudly say, 'That is a Roarke Davenport.'"

"Ha ha," I said.

"I'm serious." She looked at me sternly. "You have talent, real talent and it breaks my heart no one ever really told you that before."

"Hey, who knew?"

"You've got to believe in yourself. Know you have what it takes."

"Yeah, I know," I shrugged.

"Do you really know? Do you?"

"Yeah. Second place. Pretty great."

"Say you have talent?" Ms. Fowls said.

"What?"

"I need to hear you say it. Say you have talent."

"Relax, I know okay."

"Say it!" She smacked the table.

"I can paint okay, what's the big deal?"

"Say you have talent, Roarke."

"I have talent okay. I'm good at painting. I'm the best fucking painter ever to come out of that shit school in that shit town." I felt hot tears well up in my eyes and wiped them away quickly. I took a deep breath and tried to compose myself.

"Yes, you are," Ms. Fowls said.

We finished our pie and coffee. The check came and Ms. Fowls paid the bill. I thanked her and when we got up I felt like hugging her. Instead I just got in her car and stayed quiet all the way home.

24

The sun peeked out from the clouds every now and then like a cautious kid playing hide and seek. It was a hot and humid day and the air conditioner in my room at the Hawaiian Breeze was on the fritz. I stepped outside holding two tall boys in their six pack ring and four more in my ice bucket. I walked along the cracked sidewalk in a pair of worn out Chuck Taylor's and made my way into to the middle of the crumbling compound. A thin and graying white towel hung over my shoulder compliments of the Hawaiian Breeze. I had on a pair of cut offs and some cheap sunglasses. Wanda was pushing around her cleaning cart doing her morning run. She gave me a wave.

"Morning," I said. "Surfs up."

Wanda turned from what she was doing and leaned over her cart laughing. "Tell me you're joking."

"About what?"

"Nobody has sat around that pool in years."

"You're kidding me. I feel like I'm in Hawaii."

What the owners of the Hawaiian Breeze referred to as a swimming pool on their sign was nothing more than an eight by ten foot, twenty-four inch deep wading pool. A ring of algae ran around the top edge of the water level and two ducks floated casually in the northeast corner. The eight or so lawn and lounge chairs that sat around the wading area were brittle, beaten and bleached from the sun. A rusted "Swim at Your Own Risk" sign hung from the cheap chain link fence that surrounded the area. I kicked off my shoes and dipped a toe in the filthy water.

"Not bad."

"I know you're not getting in there," Wanda said.

"Course I am. I paid for these fine amenities and dammit I'm going to use them." I stepped down into the pool and slid down into the slime. The water's appearance was far easier to take than the smell. I cracked a beer and leaned back in the corner like I was at Club Med. The ducks didn't like sharing their turf. One quacked then they both flew away.

"I better not have to dive in there and save your ass," Wanda yelled.

"I'll be alright." I tilted my head back and felt the warmth of the sun.

"I know mouth to mouth, you know?" Wanda laughed then coughed.

"Probably good at it too." I said.

"That racket wasn't you last night was it?"

"You talking about the crazy bastard that was beating the piss out of the Coke machine at three thirty in the morning?"

"Yeah."

"Yes, that was me. You're out of Dr. Pepper."

"Peter says you owe him twenty bucks for the broken buttons on the machine."

"Tell him I'll cut him a check."

"He's already added it to your bill."

"Great, then I won't forget." I tilted up my beer and took a long pull. It was just another carefree day at the Hawaiian Breeze. "Howabout some tunes?" I hollered to Wanda.

"All I can do is turn up the clock radio."

"That'll be fine."

"We got easy listening and country?"

"Anything but the news," I said.

Wanda turned the radio up all the way. The sound was a bit fuzzy, but the little speaker did its job for the most part. Cat Stevens sang about a "Wild World" and I wondered when my phone would ring.

25

I carried my bundled canvases off the front porch of the farmhouse to the back of my car. In my new series I had created scenes from my soul, presented the verity and truths of the heart and completed works that forged both the folly and agony of life into one. Or some bullshit like that.

I rolled down the gravel road then turned onto the cracked pavement towards town. Large fields of soybeans and corn surrounded me from every direction except for the long straight line of road ahead. I leaned back in my seat and stuck my arm out the window into the morning air. I passed small farms with ponds and watering holes for horses and cattle. A double wide trailer sat comfortably on wide green acreage accented with an above ground pool and a huge satellite dish. Next to the pool a flattened beach ball sunk into the grass faded from the sun. I was excited to see what the buying public's reaction would be to my most recent work. I pulled into the fairgrounds, found a spot next to my table, and started carrying my stuff over.

"Jesus Jones, that sure as shit ain't gonna sell today," Hutch Deegan said. Hutch proudly stood out in front of his table covered with cheesy, country landscapes painted on saw blades of all shapes and sizes. He was watching me carry two of my finished canvases over to my table that sat next to his. "No offense, Roarke, but it looks like you ate some crayons and decided to shit on a piece of paper."

"No offense taken. It would take a man of your lesser intellect ten years in a library to figure out where I was coming from."

Show Pony

The Briarfield Art Market was something the mayor had cooked up a few years ago to draw tourists to Southern Illinois and give local folks a place to show off their wares. It was held on the second Saturday of every month, weather permitting. It cost ten dollars to rent a display table for the day. Macramé, ceramics, woodwork, jewelry, stained glass, pottery, sculpture, baked goods, and painting all had their own separate areas. I was most always stuck between Hutch, a retired police officer, and Kitty Wells, a hairdresser, who painted pictures of celebrities on press-on nails.

"Hell, I'll bet Kitty'll sell more Madonna pinky nails today than you will paintings," Hutch said laughing, sipping his bourbon with a splash of coffee.

"A shame we all can't be hardware impressionists," I said. Kitty laughed.

Hutch and I enjoyed busting each other's balls. Between laughs and marveling at the way Kitty's beehive hairdo defied gravity it wasn't a bad way to spend a few hours. I set my paintings out across the table and went back for three more. I hoped to sell them all that day, but I knew it was a lofty goal. Hutch walked over as I leaned the last few upright against the edge of the table.

"These are pretty good."

"Thanks, buddy," I said.

"Did you paint them with your thumb or your pecker this time?" Hutch let out a sudden burst of rapid fire chuckles. No one loved Hutch's material more than Hutch himself. He would always nod at people, trying to get them to laugh with him.

"Hey Kitty! How about a free haircut?" Hutch laughed again and pointed at his bald head.

"She doesn't do ears and nostrils," I said. Kitty laughed.

"You know what you can do with that thumb of yours, Davenport."

"Hitchhike?" I said. I had a seat in my metal folding chair and popped open a soda.

"You wanna cigarette, Roarke?" Kitty asked.

"Only if they are menthol Capris one hundreds," I said.

"You boys, always with your joking." Kitty stretched over and handed me one of her thin chick cigarettes. I nodded my thanks and lit up.

"Thanks, sweetheart." I took a big drag and exhaled. It tasted like a shaving cream fart. I smoked it down to the filter. I wondered if there would be anyone that day that would appreciate my stuff. I stumped out my butt and tossed it over at Hutch.

"Should be a good crowd today," he said, tossing it back at me.

"Yeah, what's up?"

"Lions Club got a new corn dog booth and a snow cone machine."

"Too bad they don't have a tent that teaches art appreciation."

"I thought that's what you do," Hutch said.

"Not today. Course my sales would greatly benefit by enlightening these people as to what good taste was, but then again your sales might falter."

"Whatever, kid. Your paintings wouldn't move with the word "free" on them."

"Thanks," I said.

My paintings were reasonably priced at seventy-five dollars each. I got a fair amount of compliments and some long stares. Maybe I should have painted all my stuff on old saw blades. Hutch sold his folksy bullshit by the truckload.

I was a fool. No great artist was going to get discovered at a county art festival. No influential figures in the art world ever traveled to these things. I was living in Southern Illinois for Christ's sake. Did I really think some local would have a friend who knew somebody that had a friend at the Guggenheim that would want to buy one of my paintings?

A chubby little girl chewed on her elephant ear. Powdered sugar covered her red t-shirt. She walked over and stared at my paintings, her little mind trying to comprehend my genius.

"Do you have any napkins?" she said.

"Here you go, darlin'," Hutch held out a paper towel to the youngster. "Why don't you go tell your folks how much you like my pretty saw blades."

Moments later a cute brunette in overalls and a baseball cap walked up holding the little girl's hand. She surveyed the contents of Hutch's table then looked at my paintings.

"You have a lot going on here," she said.

"Nah," I said. "It's just a hobby."

"I beg to differ. This is the work of someone with passion."

"Thank you."

"Course you can't hook one of his pieces up to a circular saw and cut a table in half?" Hutch said.

"No, you certainly have him beat there," the woman said.

I shot a look over to Hutch. He just shrugged. The brunette caught a glimpse of Kitty's table.

"Wow. Did you paint all these people on the nails yourself?"

Kitty looked up from her well-worn paperback. "Sure did." She got up and began showing the girl all her different celebrity nails. Hutch shook his head and poured more bourbon into his coffee cup.

"Gonna be one of those," he said.

26

People were breaking down their tables and loading up the remainder of their unsold offerings. Hutch and I were both half drunk and playing cards when Kitty said goodbye to us.

"See you boys next time." We both waved and watched as she sauntered off smacking her gum and counting her money.

"What'd you total out today?" Hutch asked me.

"You oughtta know, you've been sitting next to me all day?"

"Well you coulda sold something while I was takin' a piss."

"I didn't sell a damn thing," I said.

"Don't feel bad, I only sold one saw blade myself. Normally they're a pretty hot item."

"I'm afraid saw blade art has reached a saturation point my friend." We both laughed. "This just sucks. What's the point coming out here anyway?"

"You hate it so much, kill yourself."

"What?" I said.

"You heard me," Hutch said, "kill yourself."

"What in the hell are you talking about?"

"Look, you come out here all the time with your paintings and then you bitch if you don't sell them. I used to complain about my paper route when I was a kid. My uncle hated hearing people complain and whenever anyone did he'd always tell them to kill themselves. It was kind of funny, made light of how silly the situation was that they were complaining about."

"Interesting," I said. "Where is he now?"

"He killed himself," Hutch said.

Hutch got up and walked around the front of my table and looked at my paintings. He stood in front of each one taking it in then delivered his verdict. "Pass," he said. "Nope," he said in front of another one. "Nuh-uh," he said to another. Finally, he stopped in his tracks and stared at the one I had done featuring the backside of a naked woman peering around the corner at a dark figure knocking on her door. "Hot damn! You've tapped into something here, Davenport. Whatcha call this one?"

"Shifts and Intrigues."

"I like it." He looked at it for a minute or two more.

I couldn't believe it. Maybe the guy truly had a soft spot in his heart for a talented and struggling artist.

"Are you saying you want buy one of my paintings?"

"No," he said, "but I'll give you two saw blades for it."

27

The sign that hung above the empty storefront read "Bait", but around the back was a small tavern that all the townsfolk called "The Fish." It used to be a bait shop until the owner decided he could make more money selling beer to returning fisherman than nightcrawlers and leeches to outgoing ones. It was a popular dive, one that Hutch's brother-in-law owned and after the beating we took at the craft fair we decided to head over for a beer.

"Here come the painters. How'd the craft fair go boys?" Regina was the lone barmaid at The Fish. She was forty-two, single, and had a clubfoot.

"You wanna know what the problem is? There are just way too many doggone people in the world nowadays," Hutch said. "Too many people equals too few opportunities. Seriously, think about it. Back hundreds of years ago there were only so many people running around. You had your tradesmen, merchants, builders, farmers, clergy, soldiers, and then you had the artists. The artists got to make a living because everyone else had a legit job and would buy their work and employ them. Nowadays any jackass with a predilection for a government check just picks up a paintbrush and starts farting around. You know what that person is doing? He's diluting the quality of the rest of our work by having the gall to call himself an artist. It's frustrating."

Hutch and I took a seat at a middle table. Regina brought us our beers.

"Shit, Roarke. Take in the beauty of this place." Hutch swept his hand across the barroom, which was adorned with his handiwork. Saw blades of all shapes and sizes sported fishing and hunting motifs with wildlife in various forms of habitation.

"You know, those have hung up there for years. Fairly priced too. You cheap bastards," he said to no one in particular. "I really wish I knew what has killed people's passion for collecting original art?"

"Why do you paint, Roarke?" Regina asked me.

"I'm one of those mediocre hacks screwing it up for everybody else," I said.

"That and he hopes it gets him laid," Hutch said.

"Me?" I said. "All you need to be happy is a full tank of gas in your truck and a woman with nice set of double D's."

"Settle for a gal with a ten speed and a set of perky A's?" Regina said. Everyone within ear shot laughed just a little too hard and loud. Regina repaired back to the bar with her head down.

Hutch raised his glass, "as one of the most successful saw blade artists in the tri-county area, I will say here and now that you, Davenport, have true talent."

"You both suck!" said Hull Watkins, a struggling novelist and seed salesman. Hull got up with his yellow notebook and walked over to us. He looked like he was going to fall over in his velour jogging suit. He drained his scotch and soda. "The last great painter that ever lived in this country was Edward Hopper. The rest are wasting their time." He smiled at us. "Good day, gentlemen."

"Who in the hell is Eddie Hopper?" Hutch asked.

"He was in *Easy Rider*, doofus," Regina said, putting down another round in front of us. I thought of correcting her then decided not to. Nobody cared.

28

My room at the Hawaiian was sweltering. The repairman that came to look at the air conditioner decided to put it out of its misery. The new one was "on order." I cracked open the first of the six beers I had on ice in the bathroom sink. A blank canvas leaned against a makeshift easel I created by dropping down the rusty ironing board out of the wall. My tubes of paint had just enough for what I had in mind. I squirted some small piles onto my trash can lid and did some blending. I popped my thumb, wiggled it around a bit then dipped it in some paint and began.

I started with a dot of bright yellow, mixed in a light reddish brown and took the streak up the top third of the canvas until the paint ran all the way off my thumb. I repeated the process fifty times, streaks and squiggles until I had Wanda's full head of hair. Beige thumbprints made up the texture of her skin. Shading and scraping with my nail allowed me to sink her eyes. I drank the beer as I painted. Using the smallest amount of green and black, I worked on her eyes, touched the loneliness in them, the pain of rejection, and the gradual acceptance of disappointment.

So many different shapes, sizes and colors for all of us, but the way in which we burn is all the same. I looked into those green eyes as I painted them and found a kindred spirit. I didn't know the particulars of Wanda's situation, but I didn't need to. I was human.

Tests never mattered much to me. I liked winning contests, ballgames too, but if I lost, I didn't consider the pursuit or myself a failure. Failure is a word that fits in with lofty things like rocket missions to Mars, or attempts at a doctor resuscitating a dying patient. Failure is a word that leaves no other options; there is a finality to it. Failure was a word that went along with every relationship I had ever known.

Wanda, like the rest of us, started out with hopes and dreams in her marriage. She probably spent days thinking of the best curtains that would match the kitchen or what kind of casseroles might be good for dinner. Maybe a few fun afternoons spent screwing, enjoying drink and laughter. But as often happens, time and familiarity can slow those things, and the simple pressures of the day can heap up into a weekly grind. I wondered if she had been the first to start turning away from her man or if it had been the other way around.

Part of me still loved Denise. As much as I didn't want to, I still did. I knew I always would. She was as beautiful as she was difficult. While I painted Wanda, I wondered how much looks affected our lives, our fate. Denise would never work in a place like the Hawaiian, so why was Wanda? I painted the numerous piercings which hung from each of Wanda's ears. The color had fallen from her sagging cheeks and had run off with her chin. Her jewelry was cheap, the dull shine of false promises, a smile before a bad deal.

I decided to keep my motel room cleaner.

29

I met Denise at Weaver Art College down in Karo, Illinois. After my high school graduation I was looking for something to do, something beyond Briarfield, but still close enough to home. Karo was a tiny river town at the southern tip of the state that was two and a half hours away. Walter and Gladys finally had the house to themselves which also meant they were alone together, stuck with one another. Their arguments were frequent and I wanted to be far enough away to stay out of the mess, but close enough to visit if I needed to go back and help mend things.

Weaver Art College had an enrollment of approximately two hundred and seventy-five students and was run out of an old strip mall with a Giddy-Up Filling station on the eastern end. The Ben Franklin, IGA grocery, barbershop, and Mort's Dry Goods were long gone, and in their dusty and shadowed vacancy an institution for higher learning in all modes of expression was created by Kiki and Kern Weaver. Originally, the Weavers bought the property hoping to flip it to a large big box discount store, but as Karo's population got smaller and the town began getting boarded up, they found no buyers. Kiki loved art and literature. Kern was into photography and playing guitar. The two decided to open a photography studio and gallery where townspeople could come and present their art. When only two people showed up they decided to start giving classes. Word of mouth spread from there and it ended up being a cool and quirky place off the beaten path to create.

Weaver offered two-year degrees in sculpting, painting, photography, fiction, poetry and music. The faculty was a mix of ramblers, revolutionaries, fired, disgraced and/or retired teachers, and struggling artists happy to earn a paltry paycheck. The academic weight of a degree from Weaver was less than that of a gnat's nuts. Actually, with the school being unaccredited there were no real degrees, but rather what they called Distinguished Certificates of Greatness. This explained why certain classes such as quilting and creative ceramics were offered next to art theory and erotic photography. In order for one to earn their DCG, a student was required to take seven classes in their chosen discipline and three electives outside of it.

I met Denise in a poetry class. Her striking beauty and sophistication immediately made her stick out. She looked like she should be in Greenwich Village, not Karo. Her style was kooky yet sophisticated. She wore breezy, knee-length, khaki skirts, Corral cowboy boots, and oversized, wrinkled men's dress shirts. Her jewelry was silver and looked like a blacksmith had fabricated it with a hammer and a blow torch. I dug her immediately.

The class was taught by Blossom Yates, a fifty-four year old woman from jolly old England who loved hash brownies and supposedly hosted parties in which admittance was offered only if all clothing was removed. Had a male teacher thrown these parties, it would have been creepy and perhaps mildly inappropriate, but since a semi-attractive, middle-aged, somewhat hip chick with an ample bosom was doing it, it was kick ass. Blossom's poetry was bad, but her hooter baring hootenannies were a hit. Most of her students were rumored to be quite familiar with her flower.

One day after reading her epic poem, "My Brain is a Cloud that has No Rain" Blossom had invited everyone back to her place. I didn't make it.

I was working behind the counter at the Busted Egg watching some old boy crush his fifth piece of apple pie when Denise walked in wearing a sloppy sexy ensemble. "Hey Roarke," she said taking a seat two over from the Pie Guy, "can I get a cup of coffee?"

"Sorry, sister. We're only serving ugly people today."

"What?" said the Pie Guy.

"Nothing, friend. Merely complimenting the lady," I said. Denise smiled. I poured her coffee.

"Word is we missed Blossom's shindig last night. We were the only two."

"Why didn't you go?" I asked.

"I was working on something."

"How does it feel to know you disappointed every dude there?"

"Shut up." Denise smiled. "Why didn't you go?"

"Small dick. Didn't need the hassle."

"I bet," she laughed.

"Of course, I don't want to be rude so I'll make an appearance at the next one."

"Really?"

"Well, only if you come along."

"No thanks, the sixties are long gone."

"Yeah, I guess. I may just pop in for a drink to see Blossom's cans."

"Eww, are you serious?"

"Totally kidding. I hate big boobs."

"Smart ass."

"Better than a dumb ass," Pie Guy chimed in.

"Nice crowbar into the conversation," Denise said.

"You two are the only other folks in here. What the hell else am I supposed to listen to?" He slid a ten-dollar bill across the counter.

"Good point," I said, "more coffee?"

"Nope, but you can give me the address to these titty parties," he said. Denise and I laughed.

"I'm afraid you gotta be a student at Weaver," I said

"Always a catch," he said, putting his Peterbilt cap on. "Keep the change."

"Thanks for coming in." I refilled Denise's cup as Pie Guy ambled out the door.

"That name. Blossom. Ridiculous don't you think?"

"Actually you're talking to a guy who was born to a Dandelion."

"Your grandparents named their daughter Dandelion? What an awful name."

"They thought so too. My mom liked it for some reason."

Denise and I talked more and shot the shit while other customers came in and left. Before long it was dark.

"Sculptor, right? I'd like to see your work sometime."

"You should come back to my place tonight when you get off," she said.

"Let's go now," I said. "We've been closed for forty-five minutes."

30

I remember seeing Denise's sculptures for the first time. The only word that comes to mind is flow, maybe harmony. She used plasticine and would create these beautifully smooth and complicated pieces.

"I don't know the first thing about sculpture, but they look amazing to me."

"All you need to know about art," she said, "is what appeals to you and what doesn't. If it looks good and you like it, it's good right?"

"What are you doing here?"

"What do you mean?"

"You're beautiful, talented, sharp, stylish. Hell, your jewelry is even cool. You should be somewhere bigger with more opportunity."

Denise smiled at the compliments. "Why are you here?"

I held up my hand and wiggled my stumps, "Bowling career is shot to hell. Glove modeling is out. Thought I'd come down for kicks. See what happens."

"Kicks?"

"Well, that and I've always dreamed of working in a diner."

"Do you take anything seriously?"

I picked up one of her smaller sculptures. "I'm seriously curious what you're doing in Karo, IL. You could be selling your work now."

"It'll happen," she said. "Right now this is where I want to be."

I tossed her sculpture onto the couch and went in for the kiss. When the fireworks ended she looked at me and smiled.

"So when do I get to see your work?"

31

The drive from her place to mine was short. Denise parked her expensive import and we walked up the steps together. Mosquitoes hung in the heavy hot air waiting for a juicy appendage. I unlocked the front door.

"So this is the place, huh?"

"This is it," I said. I pushed the door open slowly. She stepped inside brushing against me. Denise knew a thing or two about presentation. Her perfume matched her body like khaki pants go with a navy blazer. Some women just squirt on anything thinking that because it costs sixty dollars an ounce it will work. It doesn't. You have to match these things like a fine wine with the proper aged cheese.

My apartment was a wreck. Canvases littered the room in various states of completion.

"Wow, nice shithole," Denise said.

"Thanks. I sleep under that pile of clothes over there." I pointed towards my bed. Denise walked around the room. A full ashtray sat among a few empty beer cans. Did great artists clean? Probably. Maybe that is why I didn't.

"Is the bathroom back here?"

"Yeah, just follow the cleared path on the floor."

"Do you have any wine or some beer?"

"Sure do."

"Let's have some. I want to look at your paintings."

I went into the kitchen looking for an acceptable glass to pour wine in. I dumped some merlot into a plastic McDonald's cup that was more than likely meant to be used only once. I grabbed a beer out of the fridge. When Denise returned she took the wine and smiled.

"What a beautiful glass."

"Would you believe it came with a burger and fries?"

Denise laughed. She looked at my paintings. I had a portrait I was doing of Gladys and some other landscapes and still lifes. One was a picture of a faceless man with his hand drawn back across him in a striking position standing over a child.

"Now, this is an interesting piece."

"Yes, that is the flagship from my feel good series."

"You mask a lot of your feelings in humor."

"Laughter is God's hand on the shoulder of a troubled world," I said.

"Yes it is," Denise said. "Do you title your work?"

"Some of it."

"What is this one called?" Denise pointed to the one of the faceless man.

"What Price Ego," I said.

"Interesting," she took an unusually large gulp of wine. "And you paint all of these with your thumb?"

"Yeah."

"They're really good."

"Well, I don't know about that, but thank you." I walked over and sat down on the couch while she looked some more. She held her wine like a curator in a great museum. Her right wrist was twisted around and she held the plastic cup between her breasts. Her skin was tan, but not overly so. I imagined what kind of panties she had on, if any at all.

She walked over and sat on the couch next to me. She picked up my hand. "This is one talented thumb."

"Stained, anyway." My thumb looked like a graffitied barn from painting over the years.

"Hey, but good for you," Denise said, "You took some lemons and made lemonade."

"And delicious and cheap lemonade it is."

"Any challenges you didn't anticipate?"

"Well it cut my masturbation options in half."

I finished my beer and Denise set her plastic cup down on the coffee table. We looked at each other and began kissing like two eighth grade kids pressed for time before the parents walked down the basement stairs. She moved around and straddled me. I pulled up her skirt to feel her ass. No panties.

"I want you," she said panting in my ear. She took her weight off me for a moment so I could get my pants off then slid down onto me.

"First time?" I said.

"Shut up." Denise laughed. I did as I was told.

32

Denise came from a wealthy family that owned three car dealerships. They had a nice big home, her mother was beautiful, and her dad looked healthier than I did. If her family ever struggled or had problems, I certainly wasn't aware of it. Denise seemed to have been raised with nothing but pure love and support. I had never really known anyone who came from a family that seemed so solid. It was intimidating.

Denise was smarter than me, more refined than me, and more driven than me. I learned so many things from her about life and myself. We'd go on road trips to museums, take in lectures and see plays. She introduced me to great literature and the medium of documentary film. Before I met Denise I wanted to succeed with my art, but if I didn't, I always knew I could scrape by doing something. I never really feared failure because I never expected to succeed. Denise was the first one besides Ms. Fowls to believe in me and push me.

As time went on Denise became more and more respected at Weaver. Her sculptures far surpassed any of the work her teachers had done and within three months she was teaching her own course. When we weren't painting and sculpting, we were burning up the sheets, kitchen counters and numerous other flat surfaces, and when we weren't doing that we were at functions that featured our painting and sculpting.

We had a ball at Weaver and met so many interesting people. Our first official date, Denise cooked dinner over at her place and rented Fellini's "Satyricon." Five minutes into the movie we were disturbed by the sound of a screeching guitar. Over and over again the walls were permeated with the same blazing guitar riff.

"Who is that next door?" I asked.

"That's just Porter," she said. "He's a character. C'mon, let's go say hello." She shut the movie off and we went next door.

Porter answered the door in grimy coveralls. He pulled on his long stringy beard.

"What's up Denise?" He smiled and let us in.

Porter's face was thin and his eyes seemed to be on loan from an alien being. He ran his fingers through his long messy hair. He looked like a lost roadie for the *Allman Brothers Band.*

"This is Roarke. Roarke, this is Porter."

"Yo," Porter said.

"Hey." I shook his hand.

"Roarke is a painter." Denise said.

"Cool," Porter said. "Noise bothering you guys? I can turn the sound down."

"No, not really. You actually saved me from some weird ass movie."

"Martini?"

"Fellini," Denise said.

Porter brought out a small pile of junk on his long yellowed pinky nail and inhaled it casually. A Les Paul sunburst electric guitar leaned on a dusty amplifier. An acoustic guitar and tambourine sat on the floor. A multi-track machine was hooked up on the table.

"What are you up to?" Denise asked.

"Just working on a solo."

"Let's hear it," I said.

"Yeah?" Porter asked. Denise and I both nodded.

Porter took a sip of beer then picked up the Les Paul. He turned the amplifier on and closed his eyes for a moment. He brought his hands up to the guitar and began. He started slow, playing a funky and chunky rhythm, building it slowly, but bringing up the tempo. It was incredible to see music played so well. His dirty fingernails hit the chords as his fingertips frantically danced along the fretboard. He kept his eyes closed the entire time, his hair swayed with his nodding head. All that was missing was twenty thousand disaffected youth screaming with their fists up defiantly. The riffs built up to a scorching crescendo then he rolled back down to where he began. Finished, he put the guitar down as fast as he had picked it up.

"That kind of activity will not get you laid at all," I said.

"Impressive," Denise said.

Porter nodded, "So what brings you out my way? Need some-"

"No," Denise said. "Just thought we'd come over and say hey."

"Cool man. I'll keep it down. The guy below me will be up here any minute threatening to kick my ass anyway." Porter pulled a cigarette out of one of his coverall pockets. He lit it and smiled. "Nice meeting you." He held out his hand and we shook.

"Yeah, you too," I said. We stepped out and Porter closed the door.

"He's going be huge." I said

"If the crank doesn't get in the way," Denise said. "A few bands have asked him to join but he's kind of a mess."

"That blows. You guys good friends?"

"He helped carry some of my furniture in. Made him dinner a few times."

I took a deep breath. I had already lost one woman I loved to drugs.

"Do you use?" I asked.

She paused, "Meth? No. Coke? Once. Grass? Occasionally. I'm really into a good Pinot Noir these days."

"I'm a Bronson Pinchot fan myself."

"You smoke?"

"The occasional cigarette. Pot makes me tired."

"Bad pot makes you tired," she said.

"Sucks that dude has a problem. He's really good."

"Yeah. He came over one afternoon asking if the cops had been around. I get the feeling he might cook and deal too."

Poor bastard, the women alone would be worth getting clean for. No one ever looked at an accountant and said, "Your tax deferred strategies are amazing." Only musicians and actors got that. Suits needed their Mercedes and weekend getaways in Aspen to justify their golden handcuffs, but most musicians didn't give a shit. If reincarnation was true, I made a point to come back and take music lessons.

We walked back into Denise's apartment. She turned on the movie. I wondered how a sober person could appreciate Fellini.

33

The first time Denise saw Briarfield she couldn't believe how small it was. She liked that everyone knew everyone and that the town felt safe. On top of that it was clean and real estate was cheap. The idea of owning a home as well as a place to work on her sculpting while I painted was tremendously appealing to her.

We were to have dinner with Walter and Gladys at seven, but had gotten into town early. I took her to the Elks for a few drinks. I warned her that she'd need a buzz to deal with Walter.

There was no other place on earth like the Briarfield Elks Club. With only three other liquor licenses in town, the Elks Club was the social epicenter of Briarfield. It was here that the judges and lawyers in town played pool with the same guys they put in jail years ago. Ex-husbands and ex-wives gave each other nods of hello and smiled politely at their former lover's new edition with a 'been there done that' look. The jukebox played country standards. I bought us two beers.

"Can you really bet on that video poker machine?" She asked.

"You can indeed."

"Unbelievable," she said.

Cigarette smoke from various competing brands mixed in the air with cheap perfume and Old Spice. The hairstyles were out of the nineteen eighties, but the women looked good for the most part.

"So this is THE bar, eh?"

"This is it," I said. It was from this hallowed watering hole that outrageous trysts and sexual liaisons became the talk of the town and late night legend. Young men, newly turned twenty-one, had come to the Elks for their first "public" beer and had gone home with former babysitters, old divorced schoolteachers or whomever else may have been shaking their ass that night. Public displays of affection were considered in bad taste, but the highly charged sexual choreography that took place on the dance floor said otherwise.

"Looks fun," Denise said smiling.

"It's not a bad way to spend an evening," I said.

Walter kissed Denise's hand. "Has Roarke ever pulled a fast one on you. Whatever he's promised you is all lies." It was Walter's way of trying to be funny, but it touched a real nerve in Gladys.

"Don't listen to him dear, he has shit for brains," she said. Denise and I cracked up laughing. I had never seen Gladys so surefooted and strong. Even Walter was a bit taken aback.

The place was DiStefano's Pizza for dinner. To an outsider it would seem like a greasy spoon, but to those in the know, the small Italian restaurant was considered the fanciest place in town. We sat in a green leather booth beneath a wooden clock made out of a varnished slice of tree trunk.

"What's good here?" Denise asked.

"Don't you worry about a thing," Walter said, "I'll take care of us."

"Maybe she'd like to order something for herself?" I said.

"Yes, let her order something she likes," Gladys said.

"Are you kidding?" Walter said. "This woman is our guest. She deserves the very best. Besides she looks like a salad type and the rabbit food here doesn't cut it."

"Let it rip!" Denise said.

"You'll love it," Walter said. He ordered a large jalapeno, mushroom and red onion pizza for all of us. "Let's see the poor bastards at Tombstone top this."

"What else is good here?" Denise asked.

"I wouldn't know," Gladys said throwing a thumb towards Walter. "You're a sculptor Roarke tells me."

"Yes," Denise said.

"You sell any of your sculptures?" Walter asked crunching on a butter smeared cracker.

"Some," Denise smiled.
"She has a few things in museums," I said.
"Well, Roarke is pretty broke and his paintings aren't that hot. Maybe you'd let him paint some of your sculptures and split the profits," Walter said laughing.
"Honestly," Gladys said. "I apologize for him."
Denise smiled. "It's okay. Roarke told me Walter was quite the joker."
"What made you get into art anyhow?" Walter said.
"I just liked it," Denise said.
Walter crunched a few more crackers. The waitress brought Walter and Gladys their iced teas and Denise and me our pitcher of beer. I filled our glasses.
"Did Roarke ever tell you my theory on doing things you like?"
"Seriously, Walter," I said.
"No now, listen. It's a good story, has a good point."
I squeezed Denise's leg under the table. She squeezed back. "Brace yourself," I said to her. She looked at me and smiled.
Walter started in, "So, Roarke is in fifth grade. This guy, Meadowlark Clemons, he played for the Harlem World Hoppers throughout the seventies and early eighties, comes to speak to the students at Roarke's school. The gym is packed with faculty, students and parents alike. Meadowlark Clemons tells all the kids that they can do anything they set their minds to as long as they work hard and believe in themselves. Everyone claps and cheers for the guy then he smiles and tosses a seventy-five foot hook shot from one end of the court to the other – swish! The crowd goes nuts."
"Must we listen to this?" Gladys said.
"Honey, you can tell them about your quilting in a minute," Walter said. "So anyway, after this incredible hoops exhibition all the students form a line for autographs and pictures. Roarke finally gets to Meadowlark and holds out his hand and says, 'Hi Mr. Clemons. My name is Roarke. I want to be in the NBA when I grow up.' Meadowlark turns and looks at Roarke and goes, 'Yeah? So did I kid, so did I.'"

Walter laughed then started coughing. Gladys rolled her eyes while Denise and I laughed at Walter who clearly loved the story. "Can you believe it? He sells the kids this bill of bullshit and fairy dust then cuts Roarke the straight dope on reality seconds later. Wonderful stuff."

"How about we listen to Denise for a bit, dear?" Gladys said.

"In just a minute, honey, I'm trying to make a point here and this is the tie in. So the reason I'm telling this story is because I can remember the first time Roarke wanted to be an artist. An artist? I said. Why not an astronaut or a dentist or something? Artists don't make any money. The only successful painter that ever lived to see it happen was ole Norm Rockwell, everybody else had a rough time of it until they died. Not a good line of work. You kids should keep something on the backburner."

"You're quite the art historian," Denise said smiling at me. "Your grandson is an excellent painter."

"Oh, I know," said Walter, "but my point is that I didn't grow up wanting to sell insurance, but I did it to make a living. You can't do what you want to do. You have to do what you have to do. Now, I know you kids enjoy your art, but you gotta think about your future."

"Wait a minute," Denise said, "are you saying that not only did you not believe in Roarke then, but that you don't believe in him now? Worse yet you don't know me and you say I'm living a pipe dream with sculpting?"

Walter raised his eyebrows in surprise, "Huh?"

Gladys smiled. "I like her, Roarke."

"She's great isn't she?" I said.

"I'm not saying all that," Walter said, "all I'm trying to say is that four things happen to artists. They either burn out, flake out, sell out, or kill themselves. None of those are good news."

"Oh, where did you hear that poppycock?" Gladys asked.

"Vickers kid, the one that liked watercolors, hung himself last year. I did all the paperwork on it."

"He was an artist?" Gladys asked.

"No," Walter said, "He wanted to be."

"No he didn't," I said. "Vickers died in a grain bin accident."

"Still had artistic aspirations," Walter said. "Had he spent less time dreaming with a paintbrush he would have had more time to focus on farm safety."

"Are you for real?" Gladys asked.

"Selling out for an artist is good," Denise said. "Selling out of a print or a show or a series of work is great. I think what is bad is not encouraging people, or worse not even taking a chance to do something you love."

Walter was quiet for a moment.

"Boy are you ever neat," Gladys said to Denise. Walter took a sip of his iced tea then set it down.

"So, sculpting, huh?" Walter said.

"Yeah, but we know how you feel about it, Walter," Denise said. "Let's dig into the good stuff. Tell me about the world of insurance."

Walter smiled. Denise was a hit.

34

We got married at the First Christian Church in Briarfield. It was a small service with family and a few close friends. Denise looked amazing. Clem Burris was my best man. Walter and Gladys were there and an arrangement of purple orchids stood in for Dandelion.

Denise's family was neither happy nor saddened by the union, more like indifferent. "Marrying a guy like you is just something Denise would do," her father said in his toast. "She could have gone to Princeton." Thrilled or not, they at least paid for the reception at the Elks Club then allowed us to spend four days in Longboat Key at their timeshare for our honeymoon.

We were both twenty-five and had recently quit teaching at Weaver. We found a small house on the east side of Briarfield, big enough for Denise to sculpt and me to paint. Things went well the first year. After a while, however, Denise began to grow restless with Briarfield. Small town life offered as many wonderful things to her as it didn't. Whereas, the Elks Club and DiStefano's cut it for me, Denise wanted more. She entered nearly every art show in the midwest and with her acceptance came travel. I was reluctant to enter paintings I didn't think were good enough and Denise would encourage me to stay home and continue painting for the next show while she was traveling. She'd be home for a few days then go on to the next show in the next city. I had paintings accepted at a few smaller shows in towns like Owensboro and Toledo, but either they didn't have sculpting categories or Denise didn't have any interest in their draw or geographic location.

The times were awkward and painful and with every stroke of paint I put on the canvas I felt as though it was a plea for Denise's love and acceptance. Somehow our marriage wasn't good enough for her. I felt every painting was no longer an extension of artistic expression, but rather a rushed entry to be viewed and ranked by her to see if I was still worthy of her time and companionship.

"You're a talented painter, but you have no ambition," was one of her observations. According to her, I didn't do enough to promote my work, to get it out there, but for me promotion seemed almost like braggadocio. Depending on who and what I painted, I often gave my paintings away. This enraged Denise.

"Where is the portrait that you did of Shel MacIntyre?" She asked one day.

"The one I did of him in his fishing cap with all the lures?"

"Yeah," she said, "I want to show it to a friend of mine I'm meeting in St. Louis tomorrow. I love that one."

"I gave it to Shel's wife," I said.

"Gave?"

"He's a friend."

"Does Shel roof his friend's houses for free? Does his wife cut her friends hair for free?"

"No, but come on. I was the one that asked him to sit for it." Shel was reluctant to let me paint his portrait. He had gotten his eye ripped out in a jailhouse brawl a few years back and instead of getting a glass eye he wore a patch. Sometimes though, when it got extremely hot outside, he'd flip the patch up to let the socket breathe and that was how I painted him; a black empty void in an otherwise smiling head.

"If you don't place value on your work, how in the world are your friends or better yet the buying public going to?"

"You don't get it. I enjoyed painting that portrait. It was fun for me."

"Free is for fools, Roarke. Don't you want to carve out a name and niche for yourself? Hang in galleries?"

"It certainly looks like you want me to."

Denise threw her hands up and stormed out of the room. Did I want my paintings to sell? Yes. Did I want to be successful? Yes, but we had different definitions for the same words. I also had less self-confidence than Denise did. She had no problem telling promoters or gallery owners where she wanted her sculptures displayed and how she wanted them to be lit. For me, being on the wall in a place with heavy foot traffic was enough. That people had paid to see my work was amazing.

One night in Greenwood, Mississippi at a folk art expo I sold three of my five paintings and got best in show. I was excited and wanted to celebrate. I called Denise in Chicago to tell her the news.

"Congratulations babe," was all she said. When I returned home a day later she told me what she really thought.

"Folk art? Why take such a step down. Your work deserves to be seen by better in more upscale places. Where is your passion? Your paintings no longer have the desperation or depth they once did. Contentment has ruined you."

"Being content is a bad thing?"

"Where is your hunger? Your drive?"

"Do I make you unhappy? Are you miserable here?"

"Yes, no. I don't know."

"Are you suggesting that is why your sculptures have more depth, more desperation?" She didn't answer.

"If money is so important to you, why not just open a car dealership next to your dad's? I could hang my art in there and before we'd let people test drive a car, we could push a painting on them."

"Fuck you," she said.

I went into the kitchen and grabbed a beer out of the fridge. When I walked back into the living room Denise was standing with her back to me wiping her eyes.

"I'm sorry," I said.

"Am I being unreasonable to want the best for you?"

I pulled her to me and hugged her. "Darling, if you wanted the best for me you wouldn't buy twelve ounce beers."

Our differences frayed our relationship. I wanted to settle down, she wanted to travel. I wanted a family, she wanted a career. Before we married it seemed we both wanted the same things, but I was losing my passion for painting the more she became critical of my work. When I was younger art was a joy, an escape. As I got older it became an ambitious pursuit, but I never viewed my work as a business. I never measured my success by dollars or sales or shows. Success to me was living without chaos, living in peace. Denise, on the other hand, had grown up in a peaceful environment. Her home life was happy and unaffected by the actions of others. For the same reason I avoided challenge and conflict; she needed it. I didn't want to lose her. I decided I would try to change.

35

I had concerns of burning out, but I needed my wife. I started painting pictures to sell pictures. I turned off the college football, skipped out on playing cards and painted. When I lacked passion or energy, I forced it. If I was bored or unhappy with a picture, I kept at it. I started traveling more with Denise and submitting more of my work whether I believed in the paintings or not. My vision broadened then became a blur. I rushed things and no longer took my time. Being prolific meant diluting my passion. Tired, I titled some paintings with numbers and various punctuation marks.

"Wow. I love what you've done with semicolon," Denise would say.

I was full of shit. I got accepted to more shows, made more sales. What my work lacked in pride I made up for with profit. Denise's sculptures and my paintings became like a package deal. We went to the same shows and saw the same people. It was cool for a while, but it got old.

I started seeing more of the bullshit politics of the art world rather than just art for the sake of art. I finally knew what musicians talked about when they bitched about the recording industry. There were all these asses to kiss and people to be nice to, only because that was how things got done. Denise knew everybody, all the hoops to jump through, the protocol for this and the right move to make for that. It was depressing and I began drinking more than I had before. My painting suffered for it, and I no longer cared, worse yet, I still got invited to shows. I didn't know if Denise loved me, the person, or if she just loved the idea of being married to a fellow artist. Were we inspiring one another or just trying to keep up?

One night after a show in Austin, I decided I'd had enough. I sat at the bar drinking while Denise flirted and laughed with other artists, collectors, and curators. It was amazing to watch her. It was truly a gift the way she could hold a conversation with anyone and make any subject sound interesting. She had a remarkable energy that drew people to her, made them feel good just being around her.

Two horny, middle-aged Texans spoke with her near the back of the gallery. One wore an enormous cowboy hat. I could hear her laughing and imagined her flashing that brilliant smile. Moments later she tapped on my shoulder.

"You are not going to believe this, but those two men over there are brothers."

"So," I said.

"So they own a chain of high-end steakhouses in Houston and Dallas. I just talked them into buying two of your paintings."

"My paintings? What about your stuff?"

"I sold it today."

"All of it?"

"Yeah."

"How'd you get them to even look at my stuff? It's not western."

"It's not, not Western," she said smiling. I looked at her waiting for the catch. "Okay, so at first they thought I had painted them the way I was talking them up, but then I told them they were yours."

"They still want to buy them?"

"Well, I promised them I'd let them take me line dancing tonight too, but what a small price to pay for eight thousand dollars. Congratulations, baby, you sold." She leaned over and gave me a kiss. I could smell the wine on her breath. We were both drunk.

"Those paintings of mine are shit. I had no idea what the hell I was doing on either one of them."

Denise changed from overly happy to quietly enraged. "You don't have to love everything that you put out there. You just have to convince others that you do. That is what successful artists do, Roarke. You have to play the game. It's like movie tickets and record sales or anything else. Its connections and promotion, letting people know you're there."

"Aw fuck," I said.

"You know I'm tired of lobbying for you and your work. Your holier than thou pure art shit is a mere excuse for your lack of drive and ambition."

Her words stung like my throbbing head hurt. I had been drinking single barrel bourbon neat for most of the night on an empty stomach. Mistake.

"The least you can do is come over and say hello to them."

I drained my drink. "Sure. Let's go meet them."

Denise took my arm and led me over. They were both bloated slobs that thought they owned the world. Eight grand to them was nothing. It cost more to fuel their private jet than what they probably dropped at the show. Both wore diamond pinkie rings and had huge belt buckles.

"Hi Ronnie, I'm Bo Burris and this is my brother Blake." They both held out their hands. I shook them.

"This is my husband, Roarke."

"Husband?" Bo said. "I thought you said he was just your boyfriend."

"No. He's my husband. He painted these pictures that you're buying."

"He painted them?" Bo said. "Shit, we'll still take them." He and Blake laughed like two rich, obnoxious, steakhouse chain owning Texans should.

"You painted these? How come they're not signed?" Bo asked.

"They are, you just have to look closer," Denise said.

Any painting that I ever did, that I believed in, got my signature on the back. Those that weren't my best, I conspicuously signed on the front. These not being my best, I signed them on the front.

Bo leaned forward about six inches away.

"Nope, don't see it," Bo said. Blake nudged him.

"Must have missed it by a thumb." They laughed.

I looked at Denise. She had her eyebrows raised and a tight smile. I looked at the Texans then back to Denise.

"Here, I'll sign 'em for you now." I walked over and slowly took each painting down and leaned each one against the wall. Bo held out his Montblanc.

"Here's a pen."

"Shove it up your fat cowboy ass," I said.

I unzipped my fly and proceeded to piss all over my paintings. Blake laughed at first and then stopped when he saw the splash back was hitting his ostrich boots. I heard gasps and yelling in the distance. Denise screamed something, but I kept a hot steady stream rolling over the painted canvas. I felt a slight tinge of regret when I zipped back up. The paintings really weren't that bad. Two security guards grabbed my arms and led me out. I knew the following day was going to suck, whether I ended up in jail or not.

36

We both agreed a separation would be good. Denise said she was tired of carrying me, that it was frustrating that she cared more about my career than I did. I agreed with her. I didn't want a career, I just wanted to live and paint without hassle. I didn't need things or money or articles or write-ups. I just wanted her love and acceptance, but it had to be real. I decided not to fly back with Denise and instead bought a used car. The drive from Austin back to Briarfield gave me plenty of time to think.

I was hurt, lonely, and dejected. I ran my thumb across the dash of my "new" Chevy Nomad wagon. A narrow line left its trail in the thin dust. I wondered who had owned the car before. What kind of conversations had been held in the front seat on morning drives? Was it owned by a married couple with kids, a farmer, a preacher, perhaps a moonshiner? How many careless couples fumbled drunkenly in the back seat on Saturday nights?

The chrome needed polishing and the aqua-teal paintjob had faded in spots, but the car still had its sleek lines. The engine needed tuning, but still chugged along confidently. Even the name had a presence about it. Nomad. What a great name for a car. Someone in Detroit certainly had their shit together in 1956. I gave the dash a smack.

By the time I got home Denise had already moved most of her things out of our house. She left a brief note saying she was moving to Taos, New Mexico. I never accused her of infidelity, but something told me she had a lover there. It was all too easy for her. I felt like crying, but got drunk instead. I looked at the picture of us together on the mantle. She was beautiful. I walked through the empty house looking around at what little had really been mine.

37

A few months passed and I functioned on what seemed to be autopilot. Denise asked me to sell the house. I did and mailed the check to her with a clipping about a wild catfight at the Elks. I didn't hear back, but saw she cashed the check.

I found a smaller place out in the country and fished mostly during the day then painted late into the night. Most days beer was for breakfast followed by a nice helping of self-pity for lunch. By dinner time I was wasted and angry. On good days I'd tinker around the farmhouse, try to paint a little then meet Clem at the Elks for a few beers. The way Clem saw it, I had a new lease on life.

"You still got your dick don't ya? So use it. Hell, there is more eager beaver in this town than at a Las Vegas Dam convention."

"What about the part of me that still loves Denise?"

"You need to kill that shit with a hammer. Seriously, she left you high and dry. What? So you're not famous? Who is she?"

Clem actually used to like Denise, but he was just doing what best friends do. Besides, I felt a lot of his anger was misdirected animosity towards his own wife, whom I never really liked at all, but pretended to tolerate when I saw her because that is what friends do.

"Yeah, you're right," I said. "Fuck her."

"Now you're talking," Clem said. "Besides you know somebody is."

38

Gladys finally decided to leave Walter and as happy as I was for her, I felt bad for him.

There was nothing more depressing than two aging bachelors playing chess, alone, without wives.

"I guess after years of me trying to pull Gladys' sweet tooth she finally went and got some taffy."

"I guess so," I said.

"So how'd you blow it, kid?"

"It was easy. I was myself."

"Me too," Walter said. "Do you think we're really that big a bunch of assholes?"

"No, just one of us."

Walter chuckled. There was more on his mind than the pieces on the board. "I told her to leave."

"What?"

"It wasn't hard for her."

"Are you crazy? All she's done standing by you for so long."

"That's why I told her to go. She deserves better."

"But why?"

"I'm sick. Cancer. She doesn't know. She's a good woman and should enjoy the last years of her life. I've seen a doctor. It can't be treated."

For the first time in my life I could see fear in Walter's eyes.

"How long have you known?"

"Check-up a few months ago."

I didn't know what to say. I was speechless. Walter moved his rook and took my queen. "I don't have much, but it's yours. I always thought you could have been a doctor or something. You're funny. You would have made an entertaining trial lawyer."

A golf ball sized lump developed in my throat. I looked at the man that was both a father, grandfather, friend and foe to me.

"Jesus, Walter. How long do you have?"

"Not too long. The cancer is all over my pancreas and stomach."

I leaned over and hugged him. His clothing hid his weight loss, but he felt weak to the squeeze.

"You know I always liked your drawings more than your paintings, but that doesn't mean I'm betting against you."

I looked at Walter. Gray stubble populated the sides of his bald head and the deep wrinkles and creases on his face looked like they had been pressed with an iron. He looked old and tired, but his blue steel eyes still seemed to burn with life. I could see a little of me in there and was proud that I was his grandson.

"What can I do?" I said.

"Let's just play some chess and fish together these next few weeks."

"You got it. Where do you want to go fishing?"

"I don't care," Walter said.

"What do you want to catch?"

"Doesn't matter to me."

"Well, why don't we just cut through the chase and go to Red Lobster then?" I said.

"Can't get a tan in a restaurant."

I looked and smiled at the old man. Part of me wanted to shed a tear while the other just wanted to punch a hole in the wall. Another person I loved was leaving and like being a kid all over again there wasn't a thing I could do about it.

39

Walter's funeral was four months later. No one was in his hospital room with him when he died. Though it was expected, we thought he had more time than he actually did. I often wondered if that was Walter's intent, if the old man wanted to slip out quietly without months of tears, hugs and prayers over him.

The last time I saw him, Gladys and I had gone to the hospital together. Walter was so weak and frail, but his pure stubbornness allowed him to sit up and talk to us. I wiped the perspiration from his forehead and the saliva from his mouth.

"On top of all this, the food is lousy too," He mumbled, attempting a smile.

"Oh that's not true," Gladys said. "I just had a cup of coffee and a salad in the cafeteria with Roarke."

"That true?" Walter said looking at me.

"Yeah," I nodded.

"Thanks for the invite," Walter said.

I smiled at Gladys. It was so strange to see my once strong and proud grandfather be reduced to a frail length of wheezing flesh.

"You know they spray shit yellow here and call it banana pudding," Walter said. I laughed out loud.

"Oh stop it." Gladys said. She went to playfully hit Walter, but then pulled back.

A television hung in the corner and some cards sat on the table in front of the window.

"Pretty terrific pad you have here, Walt," I said.

"Forty-five years in the insurance business and look what my coverage gets me. Pretty pathetic."

"It's fine," Gladys said.

"I brought you something to liven it up." I tore away at the newspaper I had taped around a canvas I had done. It was a painting of the day the State Trooper picked me up on the interstate riding my bike. I stood in the yard sobbing with my head down. Walter was crouched down with his hand on my head comforting me. Gladys cried when she saw the picture. Walter didn't miss a beat.

"Where in the hell is the mower?" I could tell he liked the picture, but it just wasn't him to say anything. Instead, he just nodded. "That was a good day," he said.

The three of us talked a little bit longer before his medication began to weaken him further.

"I want you to keep painting," he said. "I want you to have the storage business. It's not much, but it's a small monthly income to help with your bills."

Gladys brought him another one of her quilts and he told us he loved us. She was still angry at him for thinking he could battle it alone, but as always she forgave him.

"You stupid, stubborn, old man," she said.

"Old?" Walter said, trying to smile.

Services were held at Kale's Funeral Home the following Friday. Those that were still alive and knew Walter were there. I stood with my arm around Gladys. Jasper Sullivan was a pallbearer along with Ed Runyon and a few others. Jasper wore a St. Louis Cardinals tie.

"He was a good man," I said.

"He was a man," Gladys said.

"Sometimes that is all a man can be, himself, you know?"

"No one would ever be foolish enough to accuse Walter of not being himself," Gladys said. "I loved him."

"I know you did. He loved you too."

The minister gave a final blessing and the casket was lowered into the earth. Everyone came over to the house for coffee afterward. Some shared stories, others just told Gladys how sorry they were. I looked at her across the room. Life dealt some unique hands.

40

I saw it coming down the road a mile away even before Walter died. I thought that by anticipating the depression that I could handle it, but I was wrong. I was in a deep dark hole without a ladder or lamp and was looking for anything that might lift me out of my rut.

I went to church and sang hymns one Sunday. I tried reading the words of Norman Vincent Peale and the Bible. I listened to Tony Robbins tapes, took St. Johns wort and chased it down with V8 juice. I forced myself to paint, stood there in front of the easel even though I could only think of sleep. I would occasionally break down into tears over sappy Hallmark commercials. I was a mess. I needed help. Something to get me out of the mental fog that was jamming my creative gears and burning out my engine. The bourbon wasn't working so much anymore and Johnny Cash had run out of things to say.

I got up one morning and drove to Carmi to see Dr. Nathaniel Schilling. He was the therapist Walter and Gladys took me to after Dandelion's death. It had been years since I had seen him. I got there and signed in. The waiting room was beige and dimly lit. It was so quiet. If I didn't have a problem going in, I certainly felt like I did after sitting in that room alone for a while. Finally, the tanned and fit, Dr. Schilling, opened the door. He smiled and shook my hand. We walked into his office and I had a seat in a warm brown leather chair. I knew it wasn't true, but it seemed like some people had it all.

"So what brings you here?" He asked.

"I just wanted to stop by and show you my new haircut."

"Looks good." Schilling sucked on an English toffee and played with the wrapper. He stared at me, taking me in, sizing me up. I felt naked. "Gladys told me you're a painter, right? How's the career?"

"Couldn't be better. The Museum of Modern Art has chosen four of my paintings to go on its global traveling show and I just received a grant from the government to teach underprivileged Native American kids portraiture."

"That's terrific. So what's the problem?"

"The problem is that I'm full of shit. I haven't sold a painting let alone painted or done anything of merit in ages. Plus my grandfather just died."

"How did that make you feel?"

And that was it. The floodgates opened. I spilled my guts about missing Walter, living without Denise and all of my insecurities. I talked about my fears and phobias, my feelings of insignificance and the demons that would occasionally rear their ugly heads at night. Was I worth anything? Would I die alone? Did my father know something I didn't when he took off? A moment later, Dr. Schilling's assistant walked in and handed him a piece of paper. He held up his hand to stop me in midsentence and read the note.

"Pardon me, Mr. Davenport. It appears there is a problem with your insurance coverage. Would you happen to have a new card with your name on it so we can run it again?"

I drove all the way back to Briarfield half-laughing, half-pissed. Everything in the world seemed to be money driven. Didn't anyone do anything for the love or joy of it anymore? Do anything just because it was the right thing to do and not because of self-interest? Lady, I'd like to save you from drowning, but my pants are freshly pressed.

Denise wrote to tell me she had fallen in love with a young painter out in Taos. He was probably rich or sold well anyway. I would put my shit up against his any day of the week. I felt stupid moments later for even thinking that. In the letter Denise brought up divorce. She wasn't sure yet, but said she was seriously thinking about it. I had to laugh. You're fucking someone else four states away from your husband. I would certainly hope you're thinking about a divorce. She asked if I had spoken to a lawyer. I hadn't officially, but Clem knew the deal.

I knew it was over for us, but I still held on to a seed of hope. I knew that it would happen eventually, but even though I never saw her it was still somewhat of a comfort knowing I had a wife in New Mexico.

God, I had become such a pussy. I knew I had to buck up. I didn't need some uncaring therapist to tell me what I needed to do with my life. I just needed to build a fire under my own ass. I needed to get out of the house, back into action in some capacity.

I needed a job.

41

Most of the hayseeds, fuck-ups and kids that didn't know what they wanted to do with their lives after high school took a few classes at Pioneer Community College. It was no Harvard, but it was a place they could piss around before wasting their folk's hard earned dime at a four-year school. The place had its fair share of rednecks and mouth breathing simpletons, but every fall or so the incoming freshman crowd yielded a few corn-fed hotties hoping to read a little Faulkner or Freud before leaving for beauty school. In short, Pioneer was the perfect place for a guy like me to teach.

I taught three classes every semester: Art Appreciation, Beginning Painting, and Portraiture. Though I didn't have a four-year degree myself, my own artistic gift combined with my ability to affably bullshit landed me the job. It wasn't unusual for me to drop numerous academic and classical references from the art world into my daily conversation while talking it up with other faculty at Pioneer.

"Monet didn't paint, he bled," I would say or, "Pollock was able to frame confusion so that we could understand chaos." I actually had no idea what in the hell I was talking about, but neither did they.

If ever a teacher had gone through the motions it was me. The old art cliché was that you could teach technique, but you couldn't teach talent. That was true, but it also took time and dedication. The thing was, no one really wanted to work at anything anymore. The kids in my classroom didn't know words like apprenticeship and craftsmanship. They thought that by taking one class they could call themselves artists, that whatever they worked on in class over the course of a twelve-week semester would be worthy of hanging over their parents mantles. Not hardly. I wasn't fooled by the faces in the full room before me. These kids didn't have it or want it. They were just passing time in a safe environment.

Of course who in the hell was I? I didn't know everything. Not the important stuff anyway. In fact I knew very little. Maybe I could sit down and one of them could stand up in front of the classroom and teach me something.

I scanned the room and noticed some moron had already brought her paints and brushes to class. She smiled at me. Where in the hell did people like her come from? Probably had a packed lunch with a thermos full of homemade vegetable soup too. Precious.

The first day was always the most important day, the day to set the tone for the class for the rest of the semester. It was important these kids knew I was a badass from the get go. My formula was basically pretty simple. My first class began at nine in the morning. I sauntered in unshaven and disheveled with an enormous cup of coffee about five after. I feigned disinterest and exhaustion and wrote my name on the board in big letters.

"My name is Roarke Davenport. No mister, no professor, just Roarke." I sat down behind my desk and sipped my coffee thoughtfully eyeing my students. There were always one or two attractive females with pretty smiles and good smelling freshly shampooed hair. Nice bodies, but they were morally unattainable.

A lone male sat in the back of class wearing a Red Man ball cap. His head rested on his hands. He didn't want to be there, was bored already, and if I was lucky he would sleep most of the semester away. I made a big production of leaning back and yawning then stood up and began walking back and forth across the front of the classroom. I'd regurgitate what I could remember from Ms. Fowls and Weaver.

My olfactory senses sparked to life and sent a jolt of hope and dread through me. I smelled Denise's perfume. Had she flown back to see me, or had she flown back to demand a divorce in person? I turned around quickly and noticed a beautiful blonde taking a late seat in class. The silken strands of her hair shone like rays of light.

Her green eyes sparkled like jade and her breasts were bigger than any I had ever had the pleasure of fondling. I didn't know if it was the familiar perfume or what, but there was cute, pretty and then there was hot. This young tardy temptress was just north of holy shit!

"Sorry I'm late," she said smiling.

I glanced at my watch, took a sip of my coffee then looked up at the ceiling as though I were pondering the far reaches of space. "You damn well better be," I said. The class laughed. I cracked a smile. My star pupil was late on the first day of class and all I wanted to do was congratulate her on her thin pink sweater. "You must be, Ms. Thompson," I said looking at the attendance sheet on my desk.

"I am," she said smiling.

Her first name was Trina. She had a dark tan, smooth skin, and long athletic legs. She was holding a small handheld tape recorder.

"Okay if I tape the lecture?" she said.

"By all means," I said. "The rest of you may want to buy recorders as well." Wow! I was being recorded, this was a first. Time to shine. "What is art? Anyone in here know?" Some students looked down into their blank notebooks. Others just looked back at me clueless. An attractive brunette raised her hand. "Yes?" I said.

"It's a different way of sharing something."

"Good," I said. "Anyone else?"

"According to the Republicans it's federally funded garbage," said a fat lesbian with short hair and glasses.

"Anyone else?" I took a sip of coffee and looked out the window. No one said anything. I was slightly hungover, a bit woozy, but most of my best work was done under those conditions. "Art," I said, "is life. Without art, we should all pack our shit up into our proverbial station wagons and drive off the cliff into the abyss." I looked around. I loved it. Some were taking notes. Others were shocked as well as stimulated by my untimely use of the word shit. "Art allows us to express ourselves. To sing, dance, paint, sculpt, and perform. Art is a universal language, a way of communicating with souls unencumbered by geographic locations or language barriers. Art is everywhere. It's in your CD players, on your TVs, in magazines, billboards, museums, homes, cars, symphony halls and on stages. Not all art is good, not all art is bad. Like life, art is what it is to whoever is experiencing it."

Some students wrote frantically in their notebooks, others just looked at me. I took another sip of coffee and walked towards the windows. My beat up khaki pants and work boots were covered in drops and smears of colored paint. I wore an old cardigan sweater over my vintage t-shirt featuring an iron-on of Dolly Parton. I turned and slowly walked back across the room.

"One of the joys of great art is to discover that something so close to perfect, something so beautiful was created by something as flawed and fallible as a human being. Since the dark ages man has searched and struggled to create beauty in spite of the difficult plight or predicaments that lie in his path. It is this soulful optimism, this pursuit of truth and splendor that causes a person to pick up the paintbrush, the pen, or a flying V guitar. The fact that an imperfect entity has the will to create something noteworthy and awe-inspiring is the very cornerstone of hope in the creative endeavors of mankind." I took another sip of coffee and strode back to my desk.

"Say, man," said the kid in the hat in the back of class, "what happened to your four fingers?"

"Runaway paper cut," I said. The class was quiet for a moment then broke into laughter. Trina's magnificent breasts bounced as she laughed. I smiled at her. She smiled back at me.

"That's all I got for today. Anyone have anything they'd like to add?" No one said anything. I looked up at the clock. I was ending the class fifty-two minutes early, long enough to make it over to Donna's Café for a breakfast sandwich before my next class. "See you next week."

42

I was sitting in Briarfield's one and only coffee shop talking to Clem. He had bought the place right after graduating from law school. It was actually intended to be a law office full time, but Clem also wanted a place that made clients comfortable and wasn't so uptight. Plus, if things were slow at his practice he could still make a buck. A coffee shop made perfect sense.

"A Starbucks without the bullshit," was how Clem had described it to the local press, which in turn changed the word to "pretension" so as not to offend. Clem had actually used the name "Starcents" for a while, with the slogan "ours is cheaper," but the litigious suits from the big corporation sent a cease and desist letter and put a stop to that. Clem then wanted to change the name to "Screw the Mermaid" but since we lived in the Bible belt he knew he might turn off a few customers.

Clem had a barista drive in everyday from Mt. Vernon for a while to make and serve all the sophisticated coffee drinks while he practiced law in the back. The problem was no one ever ordered them, they just asked for a cup of regular coffee. The biscotti wasn't selling too good either, and after an old woman returned hers claiming it was stale, Clem got rid of all the hip, upscale coffee equipment, canned the fancy pastries and just served pie and regular coffee. He got rid of the leather couches, brought in an old Formica counter top, lowered his prices and changed the name to "The Drip." Within three weeks it was a stunning success.

I had a load of papers in front of me I had brought in to grade. "How have the first few weeks of classes been?" Clem asked.

"I'm afraid I'm beginning to believe my own bullshit. Yesterday I caught myself making up a word for some technique that doesn't even exist. Then later some kid asked me a question about Kandinsky that I didn't know the answer to so I just said 'he sucked.'"

Clem laughed, "And how's the Beaver, Ward?"

"I have this one student named Trina. She is not ugly."

"It's not slobbin' bobbin' Trina Thompson is it?"

"What? How do you know about her?"

"How does a red-blooded male in this town not know about her? That kid Kenny that did the tuckpointing here went to high school with her for a bit." Having a business on Main Street in a small town was as good as gossip gold. Clem always had the scoop.

"So what's the story?"

"From what I hear, she's a real maneater."

"Really?" If thoughts were movies I was shooting a porn.

"Yeah. I can't confirm this, but apparently her nickname is the anal animal."

"Get outta here."

"She was so horned up on an overnight school trip that she gangbanged a bunch of special needs kids at a science fair."

"Holy shit! Are you serious?"

"Nah, I'm just shitting you," Clem said laughing.

"Unreal."

"Ha ha. Get your hands out of your pockets."

"Do you know anything true about her?"

"Just that she looks amazing in a swimsuit."

"When did you see her in a swimsuit?"

"Jesus, man, you've gotta come into town more often. She was a lifeguard at the pool last summer. Michael was taking swimming lessons and had just learned to dive. She was sitting up in that lifeguard chair soaking up the rays. I smoked three cigarettes just looking at her while I sat on the bleachers. I didn't even see my own kid hit the water once."

"Yeah, but I'm her teacher."

"Doesn't hurt to window shop."

"She still dots all of her i's with little heart shaped bubbles when she writes."

"Sounds like a pedagogical cry for you to fuck her." Clem had an interesting marriage. One day he was in love, the next day he wanted out. After my split with Denise he told me about the healing powers of Joyce's *Ulysses*. I made it through three pages. Clem was smarter than me. "So, you talked to Denise recently?"

"Nope."

"Think she's going to file?"

"She might as well."

"Well, you know I'm your guy when it happens."

"I appreciate it."

I thought it was weird that Clem said that. He knew he was my lawyer for anything I needed. Clem tapped his fingers on the table and looked at me while I sipped my coffee. I looked back up at him and then it hit me. He wanted to know how his painting was coming. He asked that I do something for his shop and it had totally slipped my mind. One of those drunken promises you make after sixteen beers when the world is one big shining diamond.

"Your painting is coming along. I should have it done soon."

"No shit? That is awesome. I'm happy to pay you for it."

"Don't be ridiculous."

I was grateful for the enthusiasm that Clem showed for my work and was honored knowing he'd hang something of mine in his shop.

"Cool," he said. He patted me on the back. "I gotta get back to work. These homemade pies are a money maker, but the meringue is a pain in the ass."

"I hear you. Scoot on."

Clem walked away. I flipped through my stack of papers. I had asked each student to write a few sentences on what their motivation was for taking my class and pursuing painting.

Because I love art, Wendy Nelson wrote.

It looked like the most fun elective that was offered, wrote Shelly O'Toole.

My parents say I have a natural gift, wrote Macy Smith.

I needed an eight o'clock to fit into my schedule, said Natalie Gray.

I want to open myself up to feel and experience new things. This one gave me serious pause. All the i's were dotted with little hearts. God bless Trina Thompson.

The final paper in the bunch was written by the lone male in the class, Mr. Red Man ball cap himself, Herny Boone. Word down at admissions was that his real name was intended to be Henry, but a clerk in the hospital mistyped it on the birth certificate and made it Herny. His parents were Assembly of God-types that took it as a divine sign from God. Herny it was. I picked up his paper eager to see what the kid had to say. I imagined the word "Cuz" or the phrase "I don't know" scrawled in chicken scratch. This is what I got instead.

I want to be a painter, not just any painter, not one of those hackneyed jackasses that paint kids faces at the fair. I want to be famous. I want love and admiration. I want to party with rock stars, do copious amounts of drugs, bang movie stars in the White House, and offend the powerful at important events. I want to be a critical darling with commercial appeal. I want the world to think everything I do has meaning. I want the foreign press to analyze the intention of my farts. I don't just want to be a painter. I want to be a phenomenon.

I read Herny's paper over and over again. It was a boat of shit sailing on a shallow pond of piss. It reeked of self-love and importance, of ego gone amuck in a fame-whoring world. Who in the hell would ever write the things that he just did? His words were ridiculous, vain, magnificent and ballsy. Denise would have loved him. I hated him immediately.

43

It was cloudy outside. In spite of the light rain the birds kept at their songs and morning conversations. I walked amongst the sheds, sipping on an ice cold tall boy. I had planned on going fishing earlier, but once I got my cooler packed I didn't feel like running out to buy bait and hassle with my poles. Instead I decided to do a little recon over at the storage business. Everything seemed to be in order. All the locks were on and there was no sign of tampering. Of course, I didn't expect there to be. I kept the electric fence so hopped up with juice that if some errant thief tried cutting through the fence, he'd shit his pants before his wire cutters hit a piece of metal.

I walked around the perimeter of the humming fence. I made it around the far corner when a wave of panic hit me. What if Jasper tried to come out here and forgot his code? I trotted back to the tiny office and turned the electricity off. Why I was so hell bent on protecting other people's shit was beyond me. I had insurance. Where did I think the invasion was going to come from?

I drained my tall boy and walked over to the Nomad for another one. I popped open the backdoor then flipped up the lid of the cooler. I looked down and admired the view.

There was beauty in a well-packed beer cooler that went beyond just tossing in a case of cans and dumping a bag of ice over them. That was bush league. The trick was to sit the cans right side up on the bottom about an inch apart then lightly drop pieces of ice into the gaps between the cans. To insure maximum frostiness, the second layer of cans was laid sideways over the bed of ice that rested atop the cans on the bottom layer. After this another layer of ice was dumped and any remaining beers were laid on top. Like a woman neatly arranging her diamonds in a jewelry box, I took care of what I valued as well. I lit a cigarette and decided to go visit Jasper.

Bainbridge was the name of the assisted living facility. I pulled up in the Nomad, popped a stick of gum in my mouth, and went in.

"Can I help you, sir?" said a woman in a white smock standing behind the reception desk. I recognized her from my recent trip to church. She gave me a tight smile.

"Yes. I'm looking for Jasper Sullivan?"

"Are you family?"

"No, no. Just a family friend."

"Your name?"

"Roarke Davenport."

"Very good," she said. "One moment please." She turned and disappeared down the shiny white hallway. The inside of Bainbridge looked like the set where John Lennon's "Imagine" video was shot. No color, no warm hues, just white.

I heard a man talking softly, walking toward me down the hallway. I looked up and saw him pushing an old woman sitting in a wheelchair. Two young children behind me muttered something to one another.

"Look Mom, Doug and Susie are here to see you and they brought you some of their drawings." The old woman in the chair had her head slumped to one side with saliva running from her gaping mouth.

The nurse returned. "I'm sorry sir, but Jasper is not recognizing your name."

"Tell him Whitey Herzog is here," I said.

"Whitey Herzog?"

"He'll know."

"Sir, I don't know if it would be right to-"

"Look, when is the last time the guy had a visitor?"

The nurse paused for a moment. "Okay," she said. She disappeared back down the hall and returned moments later.

"He'll see you, but I should tell you first he's been having some problems as of late. Alzheimer's can really-"

"Thank you," I said stepping past her.

"Room fourteen," she said behind me.

I walked down the hall. Nearly every room I passed an old person poked their head out to see if I was someone they knew.

"No more corn," an old voice yelled from out of nowhere. I heard someone else screaming and crying from another direction.

I got to room fourteen and stepped in. Jasper was holding onto a walker and looking out the window. "Close the door," he said. I did.

"Jasper, it's me, Roarke. Roarke Davenport. Walter's grandson."

"I know. Have a seat." I took a seat in a small wooden chair. Jasper turned around and looked at me. "Sorry I had to deny you the first time, but if I act like I know too much of what is going on they make me do craft time. I hate craft time."

"Is that where your roommate is?"

"Yeah," Jasper said. "Look at that shit." Jasper nodded over towards the neatly made bed by the wall. Above it was a large red piece of construction paper with the name Myron spelled out on it in sparkly blue glitter.

"Wow. Nice work."

"Bullshit, it's sloppy. Parkinson's." Jasper stepped out from behind his walker, took a few steps over and had a seat on the edge of his bed. "You didn't bring me any corn chips did you?"

"I didn't," I said. "I'm sorry."

"Don't be. They mess up my partials. Plus they mess up the house."

"House? Who says?"

"Claire. Says it makes the furniture greasy."

"Claire's been out to visit with you? That's great."

"Yeah, she's in the other room cooking. Been married a long time now."

Jasper's words made my stomach fall. I didn't know what to do for the old man. I looked over and saw a stack of board games in the corner.

"You wanna play checkers?"

"Can I lay down?"

"Sure you can." I got up and helped the old man lay down on his bed.

"You want a blanket or something?"

"Yes. Claire knows the one that I like." Urine began to soak his pants.

"Hey, Jasper, let's get up and go to the bathroom." I grabbed him gently and tried to pull him up. He let out a scream.

"Get away from me, you bastard. Don't you ever hit me with a switch again. I'll kill you."

"Jasper, it's me, Roarke."

"Get the hell away from me. You hurt me." Jasper's eyes were looking at something else from another world. An orderly came in.

"You should go for now," she said. She stuck an IV in his arm and hit the drip. "I know it's hard, but he'll be okay."

It was an evil disease and Jasper was stuck in a horrible place. As I walked out of the room the orderly followed me.

"Aren't you going to change his pants and bed sheets?"

"After my break," she said.

44

Herny's note had inspired me to start painting again. I was hitting the canvas with more purpose than ever. Some nights I'd paint until three or four in the morning, using beer, coffee or whatever to get me through. Over the course of the next few weeks I laid the bullshit on pretty thick in class. What I knew I expounded on and what I didn't know I made up with gusto.

Only one assignment would be graded in portraiture and that was the final project. In preparation my students painted every week in class. Occasionally, I painted with them, but most of the time I would leave the room and go sleep in my car. A fellow teacher caught me once, but I said my students were having a peer discussion on how I could better inspire them.

Everything I did for money seemed like a ruse. At the storage facility I collected monthly checks for doing next to nothing. At Pioneer I collected a biweekly check for doing pretty much the same thing, nothing. Sure I cracked jokes occasionally and blurted out a few significant facts from time to time, but for the most part I didn't give a rat's ass if my students painted well or not. I'd walk behind them while they were working and often nod or make a nice comment. There were elephants in Asia that painted with their trunks that had more artistic ability than Trina, but they didn't have blonde hair and the body of a Playmate.

"Fantastic use of differing brush strokes," I said.

"Really?" Trina said.

"No, I'm lying. I've actually seen birds splatter white hot shit on windshields with more skill." Trina was deflated. Her shoulders fell and in the process her boobs drooped. Bad move. "I'm kidding," I said, "really interesting work. I'm actually inspired."

Every time I tried to walk behind Herny, he'd turn his easel.

"Herny, this is just practice. What does it matter if I see your work?"

"Just hold your horses. I want it to be a surprise."

"Indeed it will be," I said. The little prick had probably tapped into something incredible.

I looked up and watched Trina, what in the hell was she doing? She didn't know either. She stomped her foot, unhappy with her painting. I heard some of the other girls snicker. I decided it would be good to talk to her after class.

Trina was concerned she might have to drop given that she didn't have any art experience. I told her that was nonsense, that the purpose of an introductory course was to learn and that she shouldn't be intimidated as much as she should be excited to explore.

"Listen, just feel it out. Who cares if it's good or bad? It's your work. Do you think the first thing I painted I loved?"

"Yes," she said.

"Well I didn't," I said. "It was shit. My grandfather used it to catch oil from his car so the driveway would look nice."

Trina laughed. Damn that perfume. She said she needed tutoring. There were certainly a few things I wanted to help her with and as much as I knew it was wrong, I couldn't help having impure thoughts. I told her she should visit during my office hours.

"But you told Carla and Joan you don't have office hours."

"Did I?"

"So when should I come by?"

How does eight-thirty tonight at my farmhouse sound, I wanted to say. "Four is good," I said.

"Oh, thank you so much. This really means a lot."

"I hope so. I had some other cool shit I was hoping to do, but my students come first."

That day after classes I unlocked my office for the first time in months. It looked as though it had been uninhabited since the building was erected. I never used it for anything other than storage. All I had in there was a chair, an empty bookshelf, and a dirty desk littered with old tubes of paint and dried out brushes. It had apathy written all over it. No teacher that cared for his students, had an ounce of passion, or respect for their position had an office like this. Yep, it was mine.

I immediately went to work. I drove to Walmart and bought some desk items; a stapler, pencils, a holder for the pencils, a tape dispenser, etc. I brought in an old broken easel from my farmhouse and duct taped it back together then put an old canvas on it. The walls were too clean. I scattered and smeared some paint on them, flecking them with spots of color. I went down to the small public library in town and stuffed a cardboard box with all of the art books I could find then messily spread them all over my office. I strategically laid out a few things just so, fast food wrappers, a dirty ashtray, a few empty coffee cups here and there. A Hollywood set designer would have been proud.

I looked at my watch. It was three. I had an hour to kill. I sat down in my chair, propped my feet up on my newly littered desk and cracked open a book. It opened to Willem Drost's nude painting of Bathsheba. Some people really were born with talent.

45

The first time I ever saw a real live naked woman was on Halloween in the fifth grade with Clem and Levi Dupree. Clem didn't move to Briarfield until high school, but he still visited his dad on the occasional weekend. That night, Clem's dad was going to the same costume party as Randy and Dandelion. Clem's dad still didn't know too much about them so they all decided to ride together. Clem's dad also had a date. She was a young woman who lived in a small house across the street.

"You little fuckers stay out of trouble tonight. You hear me?" Randy stood with a beer in his hand. My store bought plastic Garfield costume stretched across his gut.

"You don't need to cuss in front of my boy, Randle." We were all standing in the front room of our trailer.

"Ooooh kid gloves, huh?" Randy said laughing. Clem's dad gave Randy a look. Dandelion came out of the back room dressed like a cat.

"Meee-Yowww!" Randy said.

"Be safe and be careful tonight," Clem's dad said to us. He was painted green and looked like an anemic, not-so-incredible Hulk. He handed Clem a ten-dollar bill.

"What's this for?" Clem said.

"That's for watching Melissa's boy tonight," Clem's dad said.

"Yeah and don't wait up." Randy said laughing. He gave Dandelion's ass a squeeze.

"Who in the hell is Melissa?" Clem said.

"Watch your mouth," said the Hulk.

"Yes sir," Clem said.

There was a knock on the door. A tiny woman with dark curly hair stepped in dressed in jeans and a thin t-shirt. She was smoking a long cigarette and wasn't wearing a bra.

"This is Melissa, everybody." Clem's dad said.

"Turkey's done," Randy said. Dandelion hit him on the arm. Melissa smiled.

"What are you supposed to be?" Clem asked.

"A Charlie's Angel," Melissa said smiling.

"Cuff me," Randy said.

"This is my son, Levi," she said. Out from behind her stepped a small kid with thick glasses eating a carrot.

"Hi," Levi said.

"Aww man, we got to go trick-or-treating with him?" Clem said.

"Not trick-or-treating," Melissa said. "Levi is allergic to sugar."

"What?" Clem said. His dad gave his arm a tight squeeze.

"I can't go trick or treating anyway," I said to Clem, "Randy is wearing my costume."

Clem was pissed. This was not the way he had planned on spending Halloween. "I'm telling mom," Clem said. His dad bent down and peeled off another five.

"Be good, buddy and there will be more where that came from."

"Adios, shit birds!" Randy said.

"Have fun," Dandelion said half zonked already.

"Doing what?" Clem said.

"I'm sure you boys will find something fun to do," Melissa said. The two couples walked out the door and down the concrete steps.

Clem and I looked at one another and then at Levi. "This sucks," I said.

"Turds," Clem said.

"Yeah," Levi said. We laughed.

I put a frozen pizza in the oven and we watched TV for an hour or two until Levi fell asleep. Clem and I played a few hands of UNO and Rook then raced to see who could drink their soda the fastest. Later that evening we heard Clem's dad pull up in his car. There was a knock on the door. Randy and Dandelion had decided to stay at the party. Down the street, some kids were throwing rolls of toilet paper in the trees. Clem's dad didn't want to leave us alone.

"Why don't you kids come over to our trailer?" He said. Melissa smiled and picked up Levi.

"Yeah, you guys can watch TV over there."

"What are you two going to do?" Clem said.

"I have a sore back and your Dad is going to rub it for me," Melissa said.

Clem and I looked at each other. Then Clem's dad looked at us.

"Okay," Clem said.

We all headed over to ole brownie while Randy and Dandelion howled at the moon.

Levi fell asleep again as soon as he hit the couch at Clem's. Melissa and Clem's dad went into the back room and Clem got another five bucks for just sitting on the couch. We turned on the TV and played Atari for a bit. Then we started hearing some strange sounds.

"I'm sneaking back there," Clem said.

"Me too." We left the Atari on and crawled down the dark hallway on our knees. Small rays of dim light peeked through the cracked accordion sliding door, but we couldn't see a thing.

"Oh yeah." Melissa said. Clem and I covered our mouths to keep from laughing.

"Go back," I said.

Clem and I started sneaking back down the hall when we heard a rustling in Clem's dad's bedroom. We heard footsteps heading towards the door and slipped into the bathroom as fast as we could. Seconds later the light switched on and Melissa was standing in front of us totally naked. She screamed at the top of her lungs, waking both Levi and scaring Clem's dad to death. Clem's dad came running with green paint still smeared on him. He grabbed a towel and quickly covered Melissa then pushed her back into the bedroom.

"What are you two doing in here?" He asked, peeking around the wall.

"Flossing," Clem said.

Levi walked down the hall and saw Clem's dad naked and started yelling. Clem's dad leapt back into the bedroom and closed the door.

"Holy shit!" Clem's dad yelled.

Clem and I stood there laughing. Melissa stormed out moments later with Levi in tow. I thought Clem's dad was going to kill us, but he never came out of his room. Clem and I went back into the living room to play Atari.

"If I tell my mom, he'll get in huge trouble," Clem said.

"Did you see her naked?" I asked.

"Yeah. Awesome bush."

"Man, I can't wait to get older."

I gave Melissa a big smile whenever I saw her after that. She smiled too. She was my first secret girlfriend.

46

I was touching up the old canvas in my office when there was a knock on the door. "It's open." I squeezed some paint on my easel then blended it with my thumb. I made a few swipes here and there.

"Wow," said Trina. "The artist at work."

I turned and looked at her. "Nah, just working on another oil catcher." She laughed. I wiped the paint off my thumb with a rag and sat behind my desk. "Have a seat." I pointed at the open chair I had cleverly filled with books. "Let me get those for you." I hopped up and moved the stack of books from the chair. "There you go." I took a seat back behind the desk.

"What an office. You must really stay busy. I mean look at this place. You've got a lot going on."

"Yeah, you'd think they'd give me a bigger office, but whatever. I guess it keeps me from living here."

"I admire your dedication."

"Well, passion can be exhausting." I ran my fingers through my hair. "So did you bring what you were working on?"

"Yeah," she said, "I hate it."

I took the oak tag paper from her and tacked it up on the canvas. "Not bad."

"It's awful." She caught my eyes checking out her breasts. I noticed she had unbuttoned an extra button on her oxford from earlier in the day.

"You should spend a day just working on your strokes."

"Yeah?" She said leaning in.

"Yeah. You know, back and forth, up and down kind of stuff. Nothing fancy just repetition. Up and down, up and down until you feel comfortable."

"Okay, I can do that."

She stood up and pulled a brush from her backpack. She grabbed a tube of paint and squeezed some onto the palette. She dipped the brush into the paint then started brushing her paper with slow up and down strokes.

"Like this?" She said.

"You're a pro."

Her perfume was killing me. I watched her in her skirt as she painted. I thought of Denise and her little artist boyfriend. She was probably sitting in a small pueblo eating peyote dots, telling him what an amazing painter he was, how he had vision, a style that showed the truths of the human heart, and the ability to bear the pity and pride of the soul. What a crock of shit.

"Okay, so this is boring," Trina said.

"Yeah you've got that mastered. Now try changing the widths and depth of your strokes."

"What do you mean? Show me."

I stood up from behind my desk. Trina glanced down at my crotch, letting my eyes catch hers in the process. My pulse quickened. I knew everything good or everything bad was going to happen within the next moment. I stepped over next to her and brought my hand around to the small of her back. I guided her slightly to the left so I could stand directly behind the easel.

"Let me show you a few things," I said.

"Okay." She slowly brought her right hand down and brushed her fingers across the front of my pants. She felt me harden then turned and kissed me. Within moments all of my new office supplies were on the floor and Trina and I were on my desk. She spread her legs and pulled her skirt up revealing her white panties against her tan thighs.

"Is the door locked?"

"I don't know."

"Who cares," she said. She unzipped my fly and stroked my throbbing erection, then pulled her panties to the side and guided me into her.

I pressed my hands against the back of her thighs and began moving in and out of her slowly. Our smell filled the room. Somewhere in my mind Irene Cara belted out her hit, "What a Feeling!" I extended an imaginary middle finger westward towards Denise.

47

It would be cool to say that afterwards I gave Trina a swift smack on the ass and told her she should never pick up a paintbrush again, but that's not what happened. Instead I told her out of all my students she showed the most promise. I said there was something special about the way she held a brush, saw the world, emoted on canvas.

I don't remember street signs or traffic signals on the drive home. I wondered if it all had been an out of body experience. Had the thoughts that replayed in my head actually happened? Trina's hands on my hips pulling me towards her, her green eyes looking into mine, her magnificent cans bouncing as we slammed into one another. It all seemed so unreal.

I pulled into Lou's Package Store to collect myself. I walked to the back to the refrigerated glass cases and grabbed two sixes of tall boys. I looked down and saw the remaining traces of Trina's lipstick on my fingers. I closed my eyes and could still smell her. It had happened, it had been real. Roarke Davenport, super stud, was back in the game.

"Yes!" I said walking toward the counter.

"You alright there?" Lou asked.

"You bet buddy. Just glad to see you have my favorite flavor, ice cold." I put the beer on the counter.

"Smokes?"

"Why not? Give me four of those scratch-offs too."

Lou tossed the items on the counter and rang me up. I paid and tossed my change into the coin dish.

"A good night to you, Mr. Lou."

"Adios," Lou said.

I walked out to the Nomad humming a tune. I hadn't felt that good in months. I, Roarke Davenport, had just nailed Trina Thompson, the hottest nineteen year-old in the county, on my desk, at work, with the door unlocked. Even better, I was getting paid for it.

I walked in the door to my place, danced around and sung on the way to the fridge. On my way out of the kitchen I looked over at the answering machine and noticed there were no messages. The poor little sweetie was probably lying in her bed exhausted.

I cracked a beer then stepped out onto the porch to smoke. Silhouettes of crickets and grasshoppers shot over the tall corn stalks as the pink sun sank into the ground. Ed Runyon rolled by in his old pick up and slowed down to give me a wave. I lifted my hand and gave one back.

"Hell of a day wasn't it, Davenport?"

"Sure was, Ed. It sure was."

Ed hit the gas and rolled on. Gravel popped under his tires and he quickly disappeared behind a cloud of dust.

48

The next morning I woke up like Stallone in *Rocky*. I didn't go jogging or drink any raw eggs, but I was up and at 'em by seven with the energy of ten men. I made a pot of coffee and had a cigarette. I pulled some blank canvases from the closet. I squirted some paint onto my trash can lid, cracked and wiggled my thumb and began. The strokes were fast cuts across the blank space. I moved fast, but with precision. I started almost all of my paintings with an idea or scene in my head, then just let the thumb roll. Within two hours I had a picture of Clem laughing behind his Formica counter at The Drip. In the bottom corner was a little old lady pushing her coffee cup back towards him. Her blue curls poked out from her black hat. I titled it, *This Tastes Like Piss*.

"I love it," Clem said, "It's perfect." He stuck a nail between his lips, grabbed his hammer and the canvas then walked over to a blank wall in the coffee shop. "Let me pay you for this?"

"No," I said.

"I buy the beer and bait then."

There was a dark pond on Ed Runyon's property that was loaded with fish. Ed called it a lake. I always liked to think that the definition of a lake was something it would take a motor boat at least five minutes to cross. I could swim across Ed's pond in two. Still it was the perfect size for fishing and catching a midday buzz. Clem and I sat in a pair of old lawn chairs. We broke up our intellectual discourse with the occasional cast, reel in and beer pull.

"You're full of shit."

"Most of the time, yes, today, no."

"On your desk? Come on. Let me guess? You're giving her an A too."

"It happened." I reeled in my line and casually checked my bait.

"So how'd it all go down again?"

"Nightcrawlers, please."

Clem tossed me the plastic container. "Well?"

"Just forget I brought it up," I said. "Gentlemen don't kiss and tell."

"So what's stopping you then, jackass?"

I went back through the whole story adding a few embellishments where I felt necessary and leaving out the part about arranging my office. Clem had always been a "have it together kind of guy" and it was fun to watch him actually envy me if only for a moment.

"Jesus, man, I got to get over there and see if I can teach a course on estate planning or something."

I rocked my chair back in a satisfied lean. "You should."

"I hope you had a rubber on."

"Of course I did," I said. "Just as things were getting hot and heavy, I stopped to wrestle with a slippery package and put on a prophylactic. Ladies love when a guy assumes he's going to get a piece."

"Better than getting them pregnant."

"Nah, I Peter Northed it off to the side."

"Better hope she doesn't go psycho on your ass?"

"What do you mean?"

"*Play Misty for Me*? Clint Eastwood? Some women are nuts! The prettier they are, the more their reasoning is flawed."

I looked at Clem.

"I know that sounds terrible and makes me look stupid, but it's true, man. Be careful," he said.

I laughed. "You getting any bites?"

"Not crabs. Get your dick checked."

49

Trina's parents lived in a small manufactured home on the Northwest side of town. Her father was a machinist and her mom worked at Millstone Flower Shop. Their house was orderly, neat and decorated in quaint country-style: lots of wood and quilted fabric, hand painted signs and teddy bears. One of Hutch Deegan's painted saw blades proudly hung in the living room. On top of their television was a family picture. Jake and Patty Thompson had married right out of high school and started a family. They still looked young in the photograph. They were good hardworking people. Between them they raised a knockout of a daughter and a young son.

"Thanks for the ride home," Trina said. She patted my thigh.
"Don't mention it."
"Want me to give you the tour?"
"It's probably not cool that I'm in the house."
"What's the big deal?"
"Where are your folks?"
"Still at work. Mikey's at Cub Scouts."

I looked back at the family photo. Her little brother had the look of a fourth grade smart ass. Next to the family picture was a picture of a young man in his twenties wearing a Salukis baseball uniform. He stood proudly resting his bat on his shoulder. Trina disappeared for a moment and returned with two Diet Cokes.

"Thanks." I said. "Relative?"
"No, that's Robbie. He's kind of my boyfriend, but we see other people while he's at school."
"S.I.U. huh? That's cool. Good player?"

"Leads the team in RBI's with a .300 batting average."
"Wow! What a douche."
"Did you used to play baseball?"
"Shit yeah. I was an annual all-star before they took it off the tee."
Trina laughed. "Let's go back to my room."
"Probably not a good idea right now."
"Look, I love Robbie and will probably end up marrying him, but it's not like we're married."
"I am."
"What?"
"She lives with her boyfriend in New Mexico."
"So why don't you get a divorce?"
"We're waiting to see how well this whole separation thing works out."
"Works out?"
"I'm just trying to be civil in hopes of getting some of my old concert shirts back."
Trina leaned in close to kiss me. I hesitated at first then she brought her arms around me and pulled me to her. I knew I should have walked out of there, but I didn't. Instead I stayed put and kissed her back.
"What are we going to do about this?" I said.
"About what?"
"This whole thing, this situation?"
"I'm cool with it, if you are," she said unzipping me. "We've got to be quick."

50

Classes moved on and I kept painting. Trina visited my office a few more times during the course of the semester and made the occasional trip out to my farmhouse. We worked on numerous techniques and strokes and once even found the time to paint. I had traded being a responsible adult for a selfish child. It was foolish, but it was fun. I knew we were a temporary thing, but there was something nice about pulling up to my place at night and seeing her car already there.

One night the phone rang while she was staying over. It was two-fifteen in the morning.

"Hello?"

"Hi, it's me."

"Who?"

"It's me, Denise."

"Denise?"

"Yeah. How are you doing?"

I looked into my bedroom and saw Trina's foot hanging off the mattress. She was sleeping soundly.

"Good, how are you?"

"Good." There was silence for a few moments. "I've missed talking to you."

"Oh?" I said, "Been a long time."

"I know, too long. I'd like to fly back and visit you."

"Trouble in paradise?"

"Miguel and I broke up."

"What do you want me to say? Sorry?"

"No, I just want to see you."

"Look, I'm sorry you're having a bad time, but you've got some kind of ego calling me after nearly a year of silence, thinking you still qualify as a 'me' on the phone." She didn't say anything on the other end. "Is your health okay?"

"Yeah," she said.

"That's good news, so why are you calling?"

"I miss you."

"What? You don't miss me. Go to another art show, Denise. You'll find someone."

"Where is all this coming from?"

"You left me! Remember? I spent six months wandering around trying to figure out what in the hell had happened. You were the one having a ball in Taos."

"I was in a transition."

"Some transition, you found a new guy in a heartbeat. If you didn't already have him."

"I didn't meet him until after I'd left."

"It doesn't really matter does it? I'm finally able to paint again without hearing your criticism in my head and I'm digging it."

"I'm sorry," she said.

"We've been letting this fruit hang from the vine too long."

"You mean that?"

"Yeah."

"What if we…"

"We? We haven't been a we in ages. The only way I knew you were alive was when you cashed the check I sent you."

There was a long pause. "You've found someone else?"

I looked into the bedroom and noticed Trina rousing from her sleep. I wanted to reach through the phone and pull Denise close to me like I had never held a woman before. Tell her through hot tears that she was the one and only one that I ever loved and if she ever hurt me again it would kill me, but I couldn't. I knew unless I became exactly who she wanted me to become that she'd leave again.

"Nobody else," I said.

"So this is goodbye?"

"I assumed it was a long time ago."

"So long, Roarke."

"Take care of your-" The other end of the line clicked. I sat there on the couch looking at the phone. Trina came out wearing one of my t-shirts.

"Who was that?" She asked.

"Nobody."

"Come back to bed."

"I will soon."

"Okay." Trina yawned and walked back into the bedroom.

I sat on the couch for what seemed like two more hours staring off into nothing. My mood vacillated between overjoyed and overwrought. I made a pot of coffee then walked out onto the porch and smoked until the sun came up.

51

I wrapped each painting individually then boxed them for mailing. I was entering *A Moment of Prayer at the ATM* into a competition in Milwaukee and submitting *Some of Her Best Friends are Invisible Men* and *Coin Laundry* to a show in Ames, Iowa. I had painted each one in the two weeks since Denise had called. The 'Invisible Men' painting was actually a portrait of her. She was pretty in the painting, like she was in real life. I kept the spark in her eyes like the day that we met.

I took the paintings into town to the Post Office, taught a few classes at Pioneer, played some Golden Tee at the Elks with Quint Baker then went back home.

Denise had taken everything of hers she had wanted to keep when she left. If that wasn't a sign of the finality of her decision at the time, I didn't know what was. I was still reeling from the fact that she had called me. There were still some things that I had that had been ours, meaningful to the both of us back then. I walked to the back closet in my bedroom and started pulling out old boxes of stuff: old pictures, cards and mementos. I put the boxes into the Nomad and drove out to the fire pit where Ed Runyon burned all his brush and garbage. I tossed everything down into the dark, squirted some lighter fluid and threw down a lit match. Within moments the physical memories of Denise and I went up in smoke. It was a fast burn. Fast enough that it made what we had seem small.

52

The day came when my students brought in their final paintings. As always, some were more excited than others. Some were nervous and some had excuses why they thought their work was bad. Everyone clapped as each student stood up in front of the class to present and discuss their portrait. Some students had painted their parents, others their boyfriend or friends. The fat girl with short hair and glasses had done a terrific painting of Rosie O'Donnell.

Much to my discomfort, Trina had painted a picture of me. Fortunately, she had done such a lousy job it was hard to discern who it was. That is until she started talking.

"Roarke has inspired me. He has shown me things and taught me things I never knew existed." Some of the students laughed. "Seriously," she said. "This class was wonderful and I won't ever forget it." The class gave a half-ass clap. Some students looked at me and frowned.

Herny Boone was the last to go. His mom stood in the back of the room proudly while Herny and his Dad carried in his painting. I had no idea what his folks were doing there. Were we in third grade or in college? I didn't say anything. The Boones were close friends with the school president.

Herny had ditched his hat and was wearing a collared shirt. He backed into the classroom holding the end of a long cardboard pole wrapped in beige felt. His dad proudly held the other end. The other students in the class looked on curiously. I wondered if they had seen or heard about Herny's work. I myself was dying to know, but at the same time didn't want to look. I knew it was going to be spectacular, the sky would fall, minds would open, love would permeate the atmosphere and we'd all have a deeper understanding of life. The kid was going to be huge and if I was lucky, I'd be the six fingered freak that had inspired him.

I tried to think of what I would do if his work was amazing. Would I tip my hat, admit the kid was a genius, or try to come up with some creative way to kill myself and make it look like an accident? It was go time. I took a sip of coffee out of my ridiculously large coffee mug and yawned. Herny and his dad stood at the front of the room.

"On three," he said to his old man. The kid gave the count and within seconds the future of the art world was unveiled for all to see. Herny's fellow students looked on in silence or was it awe? His mother clapped in the back of the classroom like a *Wheel of Fortune* contestant with a much needed vowel. I took a breath and stepped forward to examine the work more.

"Well?" Herny said.

"Howboutit, teach?" His dad said.

I looked at the kid's work for a moment and for the first time in my life experienced the feeling pro golfers must feel when their competition shanks one into the water on a playoff hole. There, in front of my art class at Pioneer Community College, was an airbrushed picture of what looked like a drunk Jimmy Durante in a cowboy hat sitting atop a bug-eyed Great Dane. Herny smiled from ear to ear.

"Robert E. Lee on his horse, Traveller. Incredible right? I did it all on this big piece of pool table felt. It's going on our table at home."

I smiled and patted Herny on the back. My archrival, my competitor in the world of art, had been vanquished by his own sword. While I hoped my stuff would someday hang in galleries around the world, Herny would be damned to airbrushing Confederate flags on t-shirts in Gatlinburg.

"Dynamite," I said. Trina Thompson looked at me and smiled. Had Herny's work been of museum quality I wanted to believe, I would have congratulated the kid, celebrated, mentored and promoted him, but it hadn't. My imagination had created problems that didn't exist. Herny Boone was going nowhere.

53

"Roarke?" I knew it was Trina right away, but I whipped out some high school shit and pretended I didn't know who it was.

"Who's this?" I said in a tired and aloof voice, like one who was weary from the weight of the world.

"It's Trina, dumbass!"

"You can't talk to me that way. I'm your teacher."

"Whatever. Listen, my parents are going to Mt. Vernon tonight. I wanted to know if you wanted to come over and watch *Colors* with me? I think it might be about painting." The poor girl would never be a Jeopardy champion.

"That'd be great, but wouldn't that look a little inappropriate if your folks came home early? Your comments were a bit over the top today in class."

"No they weren't. Everybody knows I have a boyfriend."

"Somehow I don't think that matters."

"You're being paranoid. Do you want to hang out tonight or not?"

"Why don't you just bring the movie over to my place? Tell the folks you're going to ride around with some friends?"

"You don't have a VCR do you?"

"You bring up an interesting point. You know I heard that movie sucked anyway."

Trina laughed. "I'll see you at eight."

It was too easy. I couldn't help myself.

54

I had asked my students to evaluate one another's work and progress in the class; much like would be done if they ever rolled the dice and took their art out to the real world for acceptance. Nobody liked rotten tomatoes and since I was giving Trina the occasional spanking, I thought it better that her classmates kill her artistic dreams rather than my grading pencil. Fearing the worst, Herny's parents invited me over for dinner. I tried to avoid it, but they insisted.

Herny was an only child, made good grades and his parents worked hard, both at their jobs and in spoiling Herny. Other than the monstrous TV, the Boone's home was like stepping back in time. Two overstuffed Lay-Z-Boys rested atop thick orange carpet and between them was a strangely carved wood coffee table with yellow glass. Their house was a split-level and pictures of their pets, past and present competed with wall space for various school portraits of their only son. In the back of the living room sat a gaudy gold and glass case that held every ribbon, medal, trophy, plaque or certificate Herny had ever won.

It seemed whatever the kid did, he was either on the winning team or took first place. I looked at all of his accolades. As a youngster his baseball team was tops in the summer, his Pop Warner team ran roughshod over everyone in the fall, and in basketball, the kid had been a free throw champ. They even had his swimming ribbons from elementary school in there. I was certain if I had enough time to search the house I'd find Polaroids in a sock drawer of Herny's most accomplished bowel movement. "Look here, he shit a perfect letter C in fifth grade and hadn't had much to eat at all."

I looked at the trophy case, all of the plastic figurines sitting atop fake marble, paper certificates and ribbons arranged in a half fan. For every kid that had been ignored, neglected or looked past growing up, there were always parents like the Boones who overdid it.

In sixth grade I drew a picture of the battle at Gettysburg for Walter on his birthday. A year or two later I was helping him clean out the garage and found it stuck under some old paint cans. He had put it there to avoid drips getting on his wooden shelves. I remember being glad I didn't work on the drawing any harder than I did. The Boones would have framed it.

We sat down at the table and Herny said the blessing. Mr. Boone started the food around. I had forgotten how good a home cooked meal was. I was putting gravy on my pork chops and mashed potatoes when Herny asked about his grade.

"How's my A looking in your class?"

"It's peer evaluation. I have no say in the matter."

"What?" Mr. Boone said, "But you're the teacher."

"That's the beauty of it," I said. "The purpose is to show the students that art and its appreciation is subjective or rather in the eye of the beholder."

"But that's not fair," Mrs. Boone said.

"Life is not fair," I said, "and that is the purpose of the exercise. The art world is not fair."

"You want me to get a bad grade to prove that life is not fair?" Herny said.

"Who said you were going to get a bad grade?"

"The girls in class don't like me. They think I'm cocky."

"Another interesting dynamic," I said. "Personality and how one carries himself can affect the reaction a work garners. Unfortunately, the art world is as political and ugly as anything else."

"Huh," Mrs. Boone said. "I wonder how your star student is gonna fare. Is how she carries herself going to affect the reaction to her work?"

"Perhaps," I said.

Mrs. Boone was tough gal. I resented her implications, but not as much as I enjoyed her mashed potatoes. I took another spoonful and continued eating during the barrage of questions.

"You should give him the grade," Mr. Boone said.

"You do realize we're talking about community college right? A grade in art basically means nothing."

"It does to me," said Herny.

"Me too," said Mr. Boone.

"Doesn't sound right to me," Mrs. Boone said. "Assigning students to do your job?"

"Everybody knows you're doing her," Herny said. "She told Carla in class."

"Herny!" Mrs. Boone yelled.

"Kids and their imaginations." I took a drink of milk.

"I suggest you think closely about how you play this thing out," Mr. Boone said. I felt all three of them staring at me.

"Pass the peas, will ya bud?" I shot Herny a fake smile.

"No," he said.

I took a few more bites of pork chop and excused myself. I might have been irresponsible and reckless in some areas of my teaching, but I damn sure wasn't going to roll over for some spoiled redneck.

"Thanks for dinner, folks. It was delicious."

55

There were few assholes in the world like Carl Balineez. Carl was the President of Pioneer Community College and wore bowties like some fat political pundit on CNN. Because all of his science fiction novels in his office were first edition hardbound, Carl considered himself to be a literary sophisticate. Carl went to the same church as Herny Boone and his folks. Carl was also an outside sales rep for John Deere and the Boones were in the market for a new combine.

"Seriously, Mr. Davenport. You know the boy deserves an A. I mean his work is exceptional. There is no doubt in my mind that that is Robert E. Lee. Looks just like him."

"Maybe," I said sitting in Carl's office, "but it's not my grade. It is the cumulative decision of Herny's fellow classmates."

"You're the teacher. You give the grades, not the students. Fix this."

"There is nothing to fix. Art is not graded. It is subjective. The person looking at it decides."

Carl took a deep breath and rubbed his face. I expected him to be more flustered than he was, but he actually seemed to keep his emotions under control.

"This problem needs to go away. We are a community college. This isn't NYU. Give the boy an A. His parents are good people. Who cares?"

The truth was I really didn't care, but the Boones reminded me of every curator I had ever met with Denise. Group hugs for hype and pretense. The privileged that lobbied always got what they wanted.

"The kid didn't even do his portrait on canvas," I said. "That was a requirement."

"Canvas like everyone else? Hell, what about rewarding him for originality? If anything I think he should be applauded for stepping outside the box and presenting something in a creative way?"

"It's airbrush for a pool table? Not an A by any means."

A wry smile crept across Carl's pockmarked face. The guy's haircut was straight out of a Supercuts ad.

"Mr. Davenport, what makes you think you are so special?"

"Excuse me," I said.

"You heard me. You think you're hot shit, but you don't know a damn thing. Weaver Art College? Please. If you are so damn good at what you do, you wouldn't be teaching, you'd be painting anywhere but here. Just cut the bullshit posturing and give the kid an A."

"The reason teachers teach, Carl, is not because they can't hack it elsewhere, but because it is a way of giving back."

"Oh fuck off, Davenport! To whom and what are you giving back? You're nobody."

"Have you been talking to my wife?"

"Speaking of grades, how about this? You sit and take a college level art exam. Think you'd pass?"

"Depends on the curve."

"Wanna take it in front of your students?" The bastard had me. I had been carrying far more chain than I could swim with. "Give the kid a fucking A or I'll expose your little affair with Ms. Thompson and fire your ass on the grounds of sexual misconduct."

"You're right, Carl," I said. "It's only community college."

Carl nodded. He stood up, reached out and grabbed my hand and shook it. He had a fake smile and his grip was limp. Whores were more sincere.

"You want to call his folks, or should I?"

"I'll call them," I said. "I'll be calling all my students."

"Why?"

"To let 'em know they're all getting A's."

Carl clapped his hands together then gave me a thumbs up. "Now you're getting the Pioneer way. We're in the encouraging business, not the discouraging business. This school is a stepping-stone, not a hurdle."

"Yeah, I guess you're right. Those kids aren't students, they're customers."

"You got that right, Mr. Davenport. We gotta keep butts in the seats. Good day, sir."

I walked out the front door of the school and smacked one of the Corinthian columns on the corner of the patio. It was a hollow piece of plastic. Balineez was right; I was posturing.

Everybody was.

56

I got in my car and headed over to Trina's. She needed to know Balineez knew, which meant the whole school knew, which in turn meant the whole town would soon know. Maybe teaching was no longer something I wanted to do. What Trina and I had done might not have been appropriate given our student teacher relationship, but it certainly wasn't illegal

I pulled up in front of Trina's home and walked up to the front door. I heard laughter coming from the living room. I knocked. Trina opened the door. Her hair was wet and she was wearing nothing but a thick terry cloth robe.

"Roarke?"

"Hey, kid," I said. A salutation that sounded wrong for too many reasons.

"What are you doing here?"

"I just wanted to talk to you about-"

"Who's that, babe?" A male voice boomed. Robbie stepped up behind Trina. "Is this the guy?"

"Yeah," Trina said.

My God, I thought. She told him. Told him everything. Other than dodging Randy when I was a kid, I had never been in a fight in my life. After suffering the indignity of having my wife leave me, my fraudulent teaching career exposed, and my tryst with a student being brought to light, I was now going to get my ass kicked by some steroid abusing college athlete. I made a fist with my left hand and stood back ready for the first blow.

"Dude, I've totally wanted to meet you man," Robbie said. I looked at Trina. She gave me some weird half smile.

"Really?" I said.
"Yeah man. C'mon in."
I did. Trina looked at me and played with her wet hair.
"Excuse me," she said. "I'm gonna get dressed."
"Hurry. I want to get the hell out of here," Robbie said. He turned back and looked at me. "That's so funny you stopped by. We were just talking about you. Trina plays your lecture tapes for me from time to time. They're hilarious."
"Oh?" I said.
"Yeah. I'm an art history major."
"What?" I looked down at the coffee table and saw Trina's tape recorder.
"Your lectures, the points you make. Some of it's fine, but a lot of your facts, your statements; they're a scream. You're totally full of shit." Robbie picked up the recorder and hit play. My voice came over the tiny speaker.
Interesting technique, Ms. Thompson. Pulling the brush back quickly, rolling it a slight half turn, then dabbing it back on the canvas is called 'quashing.' It was a modernist technique. Bet you didn't even know it.
Robbie laughed out loud and hit stop. "Holy shit, man, quashing? What is that? Pure genius on your part bro, just magically pulling shit out of your ass."
Trina must have brought me up a bit too much in their conversations. He checked it out. It was his job to take me down. Ridiculous that some jock prick was actually listening in his art classes. Is that why Trina took my class, to impress him? Make him jealous? Who knew?
"Quashing is a real technique," I said. It wasn't, but I knew Trina was listening.
"Yeah? Where? I've never heard of it."
This kid was more than just amused by me, he was angry. I looked over by the couch and saw the painting Trina had done of me.
"It's a general term."
"Bullshit," he said. "Who coined it?"

"I'm surprised given your vast knowledge of all that is art that you haven't come across it in any of your textbooks. Smart guy like you."

Robbie stood up off the couch and tossed the recorder back onto the coffee table. "Don't fuck with me, man."

"Or what, you'll kick my ass? You attack my teaching, laugh at my lectures and I'm supposed to be cool with it?"

"You know you're full of shit," he said. "That tape is full of shit. Your classes are full of shit."

So quashing wasn't a real term, so I made it up. I knew it was at least a word. Someone who painted could have used it before. It was a long shot, but my pride was grasping at anything.

"Keep reading junior," I said. "You do know how to do that, right?"

Robbie's fist came with such speed and force that I barely could see it in my peripheral vision before it hit me. Fortunately, it was just a jab. Had he gotten something behind it, he would have shattered my cheek bone.

"Stop it!" Trina screamed, running in half-dressed in a bra and jeans.

I was disoriented from the impact to my head when I felt another punch hit me in the gut. I fell down to one knee. I tried to breath, but my lungs had no air. Trina grabbed Robbie and tried pulling him back and that was when I stood up and drilled him under the chin with a left. He fell back onto the couch. Trina screamed. I tried to get my bearings.

"Stop it! Stop it! I'll call the police. They'll arrest both of you."

Robbie sat on the couch rubbing his chin, looking at me. He was deciding whether or not to kill me.

"Don't do it, Robbie," Trina said, "You'll get kicked off the baseball team."

I coughed and welcomed the air that slowly came back into my lungs.

"You're a joke, man. If I ever see you again I'll-"

"Ask me for my autograph?" I said.

Robbie got up slowly, "You smart ass."

"Get out of here, Roarke," Trina said. "It's over."

"Yeah, I was coming to tell you the same thing," I said. "Balineez knows."

"What?" Trina looked shocked by the news.

"It didn't take a detective," I said. I opened the door and walked down the pre-molded concrete steps. Then the yelling began.

"You and him?" Robbie said. "You and him? He's only got one hand."

"You've been with other girls too," Trina yelled back.

I opened my car door and got in. Teaching was hard.

57

I had just dropped off my resignation letter to Balineez and was pulling out of the Pioneer parking lot when I was hit with an unexpected emptiness. As full of shit as I may have been in the classroom, I had begun to identify myself as a teacher. As weird as it was, I had hoped the people in Briarfield had too. I was no longer just Roarke Davenport, the soon-to-be divorced hack painter with a storage business. I was an art teacher at Pioneer, a job that carried a certain amount of respect. A job that I had completely abused and taken for granted.

It could have been the three days of near constant rain, or the fact that anything I tried to paint was awful, but to say my mood was just south of cheerful was an understatement. I needed a lift. Something. I did a few up and downs on Briarfield's main drag like I was in high school again and felt like a dipshit for doing so.

I whipped into the parking lot of the Elks. It was four in the afternoon. Monte, the cook, was smoking by the back door near the dumpster.

"Well, it's RD," he said holding up his left hand for an awkward five.

"What's in the fryer today?"

"Shit."

"Does that come with a salad?"

"It does not." Monte smiled.

I walked down the hall and opened the door to the bar. Wes was drying glasses and hanging them.

"Hey Wes, is that Spiff's truck I saw outside?"

"It is my friend." He popped open a long neck and slid it to me. "*Hush Money* is in the house tonight."

"Nice!" I tossed two bucks on the bar and took a swig of beer. "He around?"

"Upstairs setting up."

If there was anyone that understood the glorious struggle of trying to succeed in creative pursuits it was Spiff Hendrix. Spiff had formed and broken up almost as many bands as he had relationships and had the tattoos and kids to prove it. Fame or fortune had never come Spiff's way, but that didn't keep him from rocking the tri-county area every weekend.

Spiff played a mean guitar and didn't have bad pipes. In high school when metal was big he formed *Death Knife*. They lasted a year or two until grunge blew up and he started *Cheddar Bomb*. A few cover bands came and went. Then one night after a number bong rips while listening to old *Run DMC* and discussing C.S. Lewis, Spiff formed *R.U.I.N. (Rappers Under the Influence of Narnia)*. They were like a Zeppelin cover band fronted by Vanilla Ice, had Vanilla been obsessed with fantasy fiction. Needless to say, catching a *R.U.I.N.* show back in the day was a real treat.

Whether his bands were good or bad I always admired Spiff. He was always positive, had a great attitude, and was convinced what he was doing was going to take off. He wasn't overly sensitive and could take criticism, a rarity among creative types. My guess was he knew at the end of the day he could play "Eruption" better than Eddie Van Halen and that was enough.

I walked into the ballroom. Spiff was standing on an amp precariously balanced on one foot. He was nailing up a banner that read *Hush Money* in hot pink letters outlined in black.

"Songwriter, manager, rocker, roadie. What don't you do?"

"If I could suck my own dick I'd be a groupie too." Spiff laughed and hopped off the amp. Other than a touch of gray around the temples he still looked like a seventeen year old kid. He held out his hand, "Good to see you, man."

"Likewise."

"Coming tonight?"

"Wouldn't miss it. Doing some originals?"

"Nah, all covers tonight. Hope to lay down some of our own stuff soon. We've got some really cool tracks."

"Nice."

"How's the painting?"

"Incredible. Probably be doing houses and barns soon."

"Nah, dude. You gotta believe baby." Spiff unscrewed the top of some mystery liquid and poured it into a machine.

"What's that?"

"Fog machine. Adds a ton to the show. Wait until you see it tonight. Killer."

"Cool."

"Hey, when we get signed, your ass is paintin' the album cover. How great will that be?"

"Huge," I said. Spiff sometimes lived in fiction, but I appreciated the thought.

"Damn, I'm out of liquid smoke. See you tonight?"

"You bet," I said. We hit the bro grip hug combo.

I got almost to the end of the ballroom when Spiff yelled, "You know if you do the cover you'll essentially be doing the shirts too."

"Awesome," I said.

"Merch man, that's where the money is." He pumped his fist in the air like it was guaranteed. Spiff man, good people.

58

It's not a cure-all, but there is something to be said for the rejuvenating powers of cold beer, rock n' roll and tight denim stretched over shaking asses. *AC/DC, Petty* and *ZZ Top* among others were all nailed as *Hush Money* was holding it down that night. Clem was so moved by "Fire Woman" and Jim Beam that he ripped his shirt off and swung it around like a helicopter propeller. Everyone was amused, except his wife, who apparently had just bought the shirt for him a week ago.

The great thing about a *Hush Money* gig was seeing old friends again. Laughing, catching up, or in my case working on closing a piece of tail. Somehow I had woven a completely unnecessary lie about a new gallery in SoHo where a few of my paintings were on display.

"I love New York. There is so much energy there." I was talking to Kara Elmsford. She rented a storage unit from me.

"Fun town for a day or two," I said like a seasoned traveler. I had actually only been to New York twice if you counted a layover at JFK.

"I've only been once. You must know it like the back of your hand."

"Not really. Just small parts." Like the lounge and pisser at the Hilton in Times Square.

"I can't believe you're showing some of your work there." Kara was on the tubby side, but had a pretty face. Her cleavage and nice perfume were real plusses. She was good to go. I had no idea why I felt the need to lie to her.

"Actually, I'd be surprised if more than one or two people even knew me there."

Kara laughed. "I love your modesty."

The rest of the night was spent drinking, dancing and slobbering all over each other like two horny high school kids. Clem and I took turns buying numerous ill-advised shots, and I remembered climbing on stage to sing "Unchained" with Spiff.

The sun was rising when I woke up. I was freezing. A naked Kara snored next to me under a pile of padded moving blankets. Our clothes were scattered all over the counter and concrete floor in my tiny box of an office at the storage lot. Kara was more plump and less pretty in the light, but the spirited bits I could recall from our dalliance made up for those concessions. I was pulling on my jeans when she rolled over and looked at me.

"This was so much fun," she giggled putting on her bra.

"A good time was had by all," I said. I hated the awkward mornings that followed one night stands.

"So you really want to take me to New York with you the next time you go?"

I was buttoning my shirt when my hangover allowed me to process the words. "What?"

"The city, next time you go, you said you'd take me to that gallery." I hated shots.

"Well, it's kind of tricky," I said patting around like I couldn't find my keys.

"Oh, I'll cover my plane ticket," she said. "Maybe we can get a room at a fun hotel." A flop sweat burst onto my forehead.

"No, it's not that. It's my schedule. I have a ton going on."

"You said last night we could go anytime."

"Really? I must have been thinking about something else."

"Okay, well let me know when. I cut hair, so I can go whenever."

We finished dressing and got to my car. I opened Kara's door and she leaned in for the dreaded morning after mouther. I coughed violently and turned away.

"You okay?"

"Yeah. I got something stuck in my throat."

"Well, we know it wasn't a hair," she giggled. I walked around to my side and smacked the back of the car with my painting hand.

"What was that?"

"Bug," I said. I fired up the engine and we were off. It was quiet for a minute or two then Kara's hand slid over and ran up and down my leg.

"Careful there. Pulled a hammy."

"Oh, sorry," she said pulling her hand away.

I looked over at her. She was doe-eyed. My God, how thick had I laid it on? "You seeing anyone?"

Her eyes lit up. "Of course not. I was with you last night wasn't I?"

"Yeah, I'm still kind of married. I mean we're separated, but I'm just not really looking to get into anything heavy right now."

"Oh," she said. "I gotcha."

There was some nice silence in the car for awhile. I breathed a sigh of relief out of the side of my mouth.

"New York Sih-TEE," she laughed. "Those salsa commercials crack me up."

"Never seen 'em."

"Are you a Yankees fan? Maybe we could go to a game while we're there."

"In the Bronx? Too dangerous."

"No it's not. It's fun."

"Heard it sucks," I said.

I should have taken her for breakfast or at least coffee, but nothing was open that early. Her failure to take a hint was unsettling, but I figured she had finally gotten it.

"I like your car."

"Thanks," I said.

"Ever fooled around in it?"

I pulled out my phone and noticed I had some imaginary voice mails. I listened to a dial tone while my doctor and a paint supplier left their messages. A fake call silently vibrated in.

"Roarke Davenport," I said. It was the make-believe SoHo gallery. We went back and forth a minute or two with niceties. I name dropped a few fake artists and joked about dinner at a fake restaurant. Then they broke the news to me. Apparently the curator had been fired and the new one hated my work. They were going to send the paintings back.

"Oh really," I said into the dial tone. "Then just crate 'em up and send them to your ass." I closed my phone and ended the bogus call. "Bastards."

"What happened?"

"No more NYC."

It wasn't until we got on Kara's block that I saw the tears. I pulled up in front of her house.

"What's wrong?"

"You're an asshole," she said. She got out of the car and slammed the door. I looked at my watch. It was six fourteen in the morning.

59

The ride down to Weaver was fun and nostalgic. Seeing old landmarks off the freeway, old billboards felt good. I hadn't been back since Denise and I graduated years ago. They no doubt would ask about her. I'd explain what an amazing artist and person she was, that it just didn't work out between us.

I had a pocketful of money in case Kiki and Kern asked me to stay down for few days and chat to a class or two. The ego boost would be welcome and it would be nice to reconnect with some of the faculty. Maybe I could even redeem my previous academic missteps and get a job teaching there. This time take the job seriously, apply myself. I would study. Learn more and drink less. Hell, possibly even meet someone. Fall in love again.

There is a slight feeling of loss when you see a building boarded up, but when it is one you've been in, spent time in, you feel old. When you see one completely bulldozed away it feels like what happened there, your experiences there, didn't even exist.

I was shocked as I rolled down the street past what used to be Weaver. I made two or three laps. The strip mall was gone. The Giddy-Up filling station was no more. A large plot of dirt, broken concrete and the random patch of grass was all that was left. The old apartment buildings were rundown and looked mostly vacant. I felt like an astronaut who had been lost in space for years, only to return and see how life had gone on without him. I dialed information hoping to touch base with the Weavers. Nothing.

The windows of The Busted Egg were all papered up. A large crack in a front window had been taped together with an intricate spider web of duct tape. A yellowed sign optimistically said "Space for Lease." I walked around trying to peek into the windows where the paper had curled. I could just barely make out the dust covered counter. The old pie case was still there.

I walked back out front and stared at the weather beaten sign. Most of it had flicked away in parts, but the orange yolk was stubbornly hanging on. I walked up and tried to jiggle the front door. For a beat up little building the lock must have been top of the line. The door didn't even move. As I stepped away I looked down and noticed a faded Post-it note that had fallen down to the lower corner inside the door. It was hard to make out. I bent down to read it. I noticed the handwriting. *RD call me (555) 901-1009.*

"Brake factory closed and that was it." Saul tossed his cigarette to the ground then stepped on it. We were leaning against our cars in his worn dirt driveway. He took a sip of his Mountain Dew like it was a fine wine.

"And the Weavers?"

"They sold everything and moved to Sedona. Kiki got into that holistic medicine and shit."

"Why'd they close the school?"

Saul hacked out a cough. "Some old gal slipped and broke her hip and sued 'em. Their insurance couldn't have covered more than a flea's ass. They sold the property to pay her out and then left town with what was left."

"And that was?"

"A few years ago. I closed The Egg not long after." Saul fired up another cigarette.

"It got that slow?"

"Hell, a dozen eggs would last me nearly a week. We used to go through eighteen dozen when you were there."

"It looks like hell around here."

"Town's all ate up. Damn meth. You gotta sign your name in a ledger to buy cold medicine."

"I bet there are a lot of people with colds down here."

"No shit." Saul spit in the grass and paced around a little bit. "Hey, so look, Roarke. The reason I put that Post-it there was I–" Saul scratched his head and took a long drag. He blew the smoke out while looking down. "Things got real tough for a bit, man."

"I'll bet," I said.

"And dammit I sold your painting."

"What painting?"

"That one you did of The Egg. Remember? I hung it over the napkin and creamer station?"

"Oh, yeah," I said. I vaguely remembered painting Saul's place. I had done it late one night on a small canvas. Denise and I had been over at Porter's place listening to him jam with some friends into the wee hours. When we got back to my place I stayed up for a few more pops while Denise hit the rack. It took me about an hour and a half to paint the picture. I thought it looked like shit. "That's great man."

Saul looked pained. "No, it's not. It was one of the best gifts I ever got. I shouldn't have sold it, but I was barely scraping by."

"Man, I'm glad it helped you out. Who bought it?"

"Some guy in a slick car gave me four hundred and fifty bucks for it. I felt like shit about it."

"Four fifty, for that?"

"Yeah, I kept telling him it wasn't for sale and he kept raising the number."

"That's fantastic," I said.

"I put that note there for you to call me so I could give you the money. Course that was then. I got nothin' now."

"I don't want any money. That was yours to do with as you pleased."

"Yeah, but it wasn't right of me to sell it." He took another drink of his Mountain Dew. "I'd give you every red cent if I had it now. I can pay you in installments. Mail you checks."

"Don't be ridiculous. I'm just bummed about what happened down here. I should have come back sooner."

"Nah, you had shit going on. By the way, how's that good lookin' woman of yours?"

"Denise? She's good. We're not together anymore, but she's good."

Saul let out whistle, "Damn. She was something."

"She was."

"You'll never find one like that again," Saul said.

"Hope not."

Saul laughed. "Shit. Hot and crazy go hand in hand. It's God's way of evening things out."

"You dated your fair share of insane tens have you Saul?"

"No, but I took a bonkers five to dinner once and she tried to stab me when I ate the last McNugget." He slapped me on the arm.

We talked a bit more. I even drank one of Saul's Mountain Dews. He said he hadn't worked in over a year and was pulling a disability check from a dubious roofing accident. A bad joke and a handshake later I was backing down his drive.

"Hey, maybe I'll come up one of these days and we can get fucked up." Saul yelled. He had a big smile and a cigarette dangled from of his mouth. "It'll be on me with your picture money."

I let out a fake laugh and gave a wave. I felt like I wanted to die.

60

I sat on the couch in my rented farm house watching TV. I drained a tall boy and watched a paid promo spot for an omelet maker that could apparently cook everything under the sun. Whatever the old red headed gal tossed into the tiny pan, the dude doing the commercial with her would nearly cream his pants when he took a bite.

"You mean you just tossed in a can of soup, two pieces of stale bread, some beef jerky and now I'm enjoying this incredible lasagna?"

"Yep. That's all I did, Todd, and that is all our viewers will need to do too when they buy this phenomenal machine."

After that was over another ad came on. Two cheesy looking twins were hawking their card counting system and gambling strategies. Anyone could do it they said, all it took was three hundred and fifty dollars for their *Power Wagering Program* and you were on your way. The cover of their training materials looked like a movie poster for a romantic teen comedy from the 80's. Both guys had on cheap suits, and leaned against the sides of a polished Bentley. They had their backs to one another and looked over their shoulders smiling at the camera.

I flipped off the TV and tossed the remote onto the coffee table. I got up and began cleaning the place. Trash, food containers, old newspapers, empty bottles all got tossed. I did laundry, folded clothes. I tore through the house like a tornado. I wiped down counters, swept, even ran the vacuum. If those two cats could make it, why couldn't I? I sold paintings when I was with Denise. I could do it again.

I took a long hot shower and meditated in the steam. I thought of calling Kara or dropping her a note. Maybe I'd just lay it bare. Tell her the truth; that I was adrift on a rudderless ship built on a cheap beer buzz and self pity. My lies to her weren't so much to pick her up as much as they were to pick me up. A success I imagined for myself, a success I could feel if I actually stepped up to the plate and took a swing instead of stepping into the path of ball.

61

I was sleeping in my room at the Hawaiian when my phone rang. It was Clem. Denise had signed the divorce papers.

"And the storage units?"

"Deegan dropped by to pick up the keys. He said he'll wire the payment in installments like we discussed. Unless, you'll take a few saw blades in trade." I laughed, thanked Clem, and hung up the phone.

I looked at the picture I had painted of Wanda. She wore her pain and disappointment like wet heavy clothing, but still had something in her eyes. Maybe it was laughter at the folly of life. Maybe even hope. I took down the cheap art deco print from the wall and hung Wanda's portrait in its place. On the back I had signed it: *To Wanda, Free is For Fools. - Roarke Davenport.*

I loaded up my stuff and got into the Nomad. There were over two hundred art galleries in New York City. I turned onto Highway 41 and watched the speedometer climb.